THE LAST TIME I DIED

JOE NELMS

TYRUS
BOOKS
F+W Media, Inc.

Published by
TYRUS BOOKS
an imprint of F+W Media, Inc.
10151 Carver Road, Suite 200
Blue Ash, OH 45242. U.S.A.
www.tyrusbooks.com

ISBN 10: 1-4405-7180-5
ISBN 13: 978-1-4405-7180-0
eISBN 10: 1-4405-7181-3
eISBN 13: 978-1-4405-7181-7

Printed in the United States of America.

10 9 8 7 6 5 4 3 2 1

Library of Congress Cataloging-in-Publication Data

Nelms, Joe.
  The last time I died / Joe Nelms.
    p. cm.
  ISBN 13: 978-1-4405-7180-0 -- ISBN 10: 1-4405-7180-5 -- eISBN 13: 978-1-4405-7181-7
-- eISBN 10: 1-4405-7181-3
  I. Title.
  PS3614.E4443L38 2014
  813'6--dc23

                        2013031038

This book is available at quantity discounts for bulk purchases.
For information, please call 1-800-289-0963.

For Amy, Zoe, and Rufus

Ultimately, a thing exists only by virtue of its boundaries.

—Robert Musil

1

Black.

Time to die.

The average response time of an ambulance in Manhattan is six minutes and thirteen seconds. I'll wait two and a half minutes after I make my call.

I carefully position my feet in the center of the chair. Fucking modern design looks great, but it will tip in a heartbeat if you're not careful.

The noose is tied to the exposed water pipe I used to do chin-ups on to impress Lisa, so I know it will hold.

My apartment door is slightly ajar and clearly marked 4B as in boy.

The front door of the building is propped open with a doorstop and I've taped a sign on it asking my neighbors for their patience while I move a sofa.

I drop the meticulously tied rope around my neck, positioning it so that it will most likely not cause any vertebrae to crack. The best you can do in this situation is play the odds and hope for the best.

Nine. One. One.

—Hi, I'd like to report an attempted suicide. Would you please send an ambulance to one thirteen Prince street, apartment seven B, as in boy. . . . That's correct, 'boy.' Thank you. Oh, and please hurry. . . . No, I can't.

I hang up, toss the phone onto the couch, and check my watch. Two minutes and twenty five seconds to go.

2

(Please be forewarned: This is no hagiography.)

The gentleman under consideration is inarguably a lout.

An ogre.

A peddler of the most garrulous of hokum with an unsavory penchant for self-indulgent masochism.

But here you are. The old boy has been standing at the ready for a good two minutes and you have yet to say a word. The suspense is delicious.

You watch. Taking in every sacred detail. Unable to move your naive little gaze from his shoes. You don't dare chance missing the most thrilling microseconds of the day, do you? After all, when our man's feet leave the chair on which he is so precariously perched the story is over.

Or is it?

Never you mind. Let me reiterate. The old boy isn't worth your time. He is no one.

Two weeks earlier.

3

(Pay no attention to the insufferable chap at the furthest end of the bar.)

He's less likely to notice you if your eyes are averted and, please pay closest attention when I caution you, that guideline should be of the utmost priority this evening.

In a matter of moments the scoundrel will be attempting some form of attention-garnering stunt likely involving a lurid confrontation, pernicious vandalism, or the expulsion of bodily fluids around and/or onto his neighboring patrons.

So, you'd rather he didn't focus his weary eyes on you before then.

It is my personal and passionate recommendation that you skip your pre-dinner cocktail and make your way directly to your table or, better still, leave the restaurant entirely.

For now, he simmers.

Should you find yourself caught in the funnel of this jackanapes's gormless gimcrackery, do try to avoid regarding his comportment a personal attack. Your transgressor is a man who suffers from an overabundance of stress and is ignorant of the proper means with which to diffuse it.

For the record, he is thirty-eight years of age.

Our man has pointedly taken advantage of the last hour to self-medicate with a gratuitously pretentious vodka, although, in all candor, he would have settled for tub gin. Those of you who dare observe his falling face as he scans the room in the mirror behind the bar may find what you think is hope or vulnerability. It might be. Careful, though. What you will also find in those eyes is seditious monkeyshine. A lure for compassionate naïfs such as yourself. He cannot help himself.

To the casual observer, this is a calm trifle of a man easily overlooked. A crumpled little scab hunkered down in a world to which he might not completely belong.

Pity him, if you must. But also know that he's as calculated a hunter as there exists.

Cunning. Bloodthirsty. Wounded.

Sometimes his attacks are savage and obvious. Other occasions they are subtle and infuriating. Tonight, so far, they are self-inflicted.

Ah me, here we go.

The gentleman behind the bar glides over to inquire about our man's status. His voice, low but audible, respectfully offers to tally the evening's charges. It is a less than subtle indication that our man has quietly been determined over-served.

Our man's response is predictable, if slurred.

—Another martini.

—I'm sorry, sir. I don't think that's a good idea.

The game is afoot. Our man lifts his heavy, heavy head to meet the sharp, sober eyes in front of him.

—Hey, just because you like blowing my father doesn't make you my mother. Pour my fucking drink.

The bartender's reaction is a polished and practiced one. It is practically invisible. He nods to a manager across the room who whispers to a waiter next to him who speaks calmly to another, more sizable waiter passing by and that is that.

Within forty-five seconds our man has been efficiently escorted out of the restaurant and unceremoniously deposited onto the cold Manhattan sidewalk to fend for himself. He is advised to avoid the premises for the foreseeable future and observed for the brief moments it takes for him to careen down the block far enough to assuage any and all attending eyes that he is gone for the evening.

Well done, old boy. Mission accomplished.

4

Traffic is flying down Sixth Avenue tonight.

Well, flying might be an exaggeration, but for this time of night in midtown? Not bad. A steady stream of thirty miles an hour. It's the honking that bugs me. I'm trying to think.

Lisa fought for me. She tried everything. Begged me to work with her. Begged. That seemed so odd to me. Didn't we fall in love without even trying? Honestly, I remember being kind of aggravated that it happened. I was having such a good time as a single man when this giant lightning bolt hits me and she's all I think about and I can't help myself. I didn't have a choice but to fall in love. So why did I have to work at marriage?

A black guy in a produce truck yells at me. If I heard him correctly, he thinks I'm an idiot. A *fucking* idiot, to clarify. Alright, fair enough. But you're the one driving that junker on third shift.

I feel like marriage should have been a self-perpetuating machine. Everyone always warned me that you had to really work at it. You have to work at it but it's worth it. I assumed they were telling me that because they thought I was a selfish bastard who wasn't ready for commitment. I said I would work with her but I never did.

I lied.

—Asshole!

The headlights are blinding. And they won't stop coming. I put my hands up to block my eyes but then I can't see where I'm going. The cars whoosh by so fast some of them don't even notice me until they've already passed. I watch a few of the drivers' eyes widen as they approach. Steady on, people. Nothing to see here.

—Move, dick!

You have to think long-term about relationships. Here's the tradeoff you need to make peace with: What if you open your soul and then, later on, things don't work out? What if you make the effort and everything that you are is laid bare for someone to see and soak up and then they have that forever? It's not like you can ask for your deepest, darkest secrets back, is it? They are now a shared possession and you have to have trust that proper care will be taken of them. But that never happens, does it? Some secrets are too good to keep quiet for too long. Time and distance create a fog of emotional safety around your chosen secret keepers. In the mind of those who don't live with these hidden treasures every god damn day of their life, the sting seems to soften a bit over time. They evolve from shocking revelations into novelty facts. And revealing them seems less like a shattering of sacred bond and more like a parlor trick. And who doesn't like parlor tricks?

Don't ever say anything, but . . .

Between you and me . . .

You're not going to believe this . . .

At first the betrayal is a bit of a rush. A tiny shot of adrenaline, the knowledge that they're killing someone just a little bit by opening their fat mouth. It's inevitably couched with *Keep this quiet, okay?* and *If you tell anyone I'll kill you!* but they're still doing exactly what you were terrified they would do before you trusted them anyway. You'll never know, of course. That relationship has long disintegrated and you've both moved on.

—What are you, crazy?!

A livery driver in a turban slows his roll long enough to tell me to get the fuck out of the middle of the street. What, does he own the road? I'm a taxpayer, too.

You can't hurt me.

I spread my arms like wings and smile as I walk. Everyone stay in your lane and you'll be fine.

Looking back on the ruins of my marriage with some perspective, yes, I might have done some things different. Opened up. Shared. Listened. But it's always easy to see that stuff when it's too late. Ultimately, I blame myself. But that shouldn't be a surprise. So does everyone else.

A thoughtful driver in an SUV yells something about me getting killed.

Nice try, sucka. I'm already dead.

5

*It's four years ago.

I'm sitting at dinner with friends I've since let drift away.

It's the first warm night of spring and we're celebrating someone or something or nothing with an al fresco meal. I am what I remember as happy.

An old girlfriend walks up. Dana. We parted on good terms a while ago and remained friends, so I don't mind the interruption. She saw us from inside the restaurant. At the bar waiting for the table she was never going to get.

She's with a friend.

I welcome the opportunity to add new possibilities to the evening's mix, but Dana's with a girl I can already tell is a pain in the ass. She's too beautiful and her hair is perfect. Look at that skin. Jesus.

You always want a little something to be off even if it's only a little bit. You want to know she knows she's human. Not the case with this one. From what I can tell in the first five seconds I'm in her presence, she's flawless. Her body is Pilates-ed to within an inch of its life and the little black dress she's poured herself into fits like it's trying to impress her.

The tip-off is the shoes.

In those heels I bet she can't walk more than the distance between the cab that brought her here and the bar. High maintenance. Trouble. God help the man who gets in her way when she's trying on outfits.

Dana and her friend squeeze into our table as if we'd invited them. The friend's eyes meet mine briefly, but long enough for me to know I've been assessed as well.

She introduces herself around and makes it a point not to spend too much time on me in the process. I can see we've got an issue already. She's at the far end of a table for six and it feels like our chairs are pulling toward each other. I'm careful about how much I direct any conversation her way. Wouldn't want to give the wrong impression. On her end, she's playing things very cool as well. Focusing her attention on my married friend, David. Turns out they're in similar businesses. He in advertising, she in fashion. She's well spoken and so effortlessly confident. They're discussing photographers and designers I've never heard of.

She lives uptown.

She's from Philadelphia.

She speaks fluent French.

She's an avid reader.

Democrat.

Former downtown music scene fixture.

Ran the marathon last year.

Cooks.

I'm having trouble keeping up with the conversation on my end of the table because I'm listening so intently to hers and I'm afraid it's going to be obvious soon. I force myself to concentrate on whatever the fuck David's wife is telling me but really I don't care at all and find myself making sure my head is held just so, in case the high-maintenance pain in the ass looks my way.

I'm a distracted peacock.

Fucking wish I'd worn the blue shirt. Why didn't I wear the blue shirt? My eye color shifts between green and blue depending on what I wear. When I wear green, they turn green. When I wear blue, they turn blue. I'm wearing white. I would look so much better if my eyes were blue right now but I didn't wear the god damn blue shirt. I should put more thought into this kind of thing and it's too late to fix it now. At least I got a haircut last week. Maybe I had a premonition.

I catch myself getting caught up in my own bizarre magical thinking and insist that I return to the real world. Look at the menu. Order a drink. Check out the waitress's ass. Do something besides fret and posture like an eighth-grade girl.

We order, we drink, we laugh. I drink a little more than I should. I say maybe three sentences to her the whole dinner, calling her bluff. She's got a smile that makes you want to do things for her.

She's driving me nuts. I happen to know I'm being funny this night but she's not buying any of it. Giving me nothing. Anything that comes out of my mouth and wafts her direction sours before it hits her.

Despite my best efforts I'm sketching a composite of her personality and the life she leads when she's not around me.

Farmers' market on Saturdays.

Works in Tribeca.

Spinning class.

Hates to travel.

No pets.

Really funny.

I can't stop.

The older woman at the next table makes it a point to lean over and compliment the pain in the ass on how delicious her perfume smells. She's not wrong. The scent reminds me of somewhere I'd rather be.

We pay the check and start the debate of where to head next. Of utmost concern to me is steering the thinking toward whatever destination will be of most interest to the pain in the ass. If we drink a little more in the right environment, who knows where the evening might lead? I want her to go with us, but I know the best thing that could happen is that she decides to call it an early night and leave. Or she remembers some other plans she has. Or she meets another guy and splinters off from us. Something that gets me off the hook. But none of these things happen and we decide on margaritas across the street.

Her name is Lisa.

I know already this will not be good.

I wake up with another wicked hangover compounded by a whirlwind of half-memories from the previous evening.

Yelling at Lisa.

Martinis.

A bullshit fight with a bunch of waiters.

Something about a cab driver and Sixth Avenue and all those fucking horns.

My leg hurts but I have no idea why.

If I had my druthers I'd never wake up. I'd stay in the black of REM where there's nothing and nobody. Like I deserve.

A shower. A shave. Some coffee with enough scotch to take the god damn edge off. My head buzzes and it makes the coffee taste extra bitter. I don't even remember making it this morning. I sit on the bed for a good fifteen minutes thinking of nothing as I stare at the back of my open closet. What if I never moved from this spot? Wouldn't be the worst thing that ever happened.

Every morning I'm extinguished but somehow still walking. If I had the initiative to try, I would have to work my way up to usefulness.

Finally, I stand and slide my jacket on. At least I look the part of a capable lawyer. A capable lawyer ten years older than I actually am.

My keys must be somewhere. I dig through the suit I wore last night. There's blood on the lapel. I find them in the front pocket for some reason. Lucky break.

One more cup of coffee as I gather my thoughts.

I am a cancer of me. I want to suck myself into the black hole of my mind and I want to take you with me.

There's a stack of unopened mail on the kitchen counter. I should pay those bills. The stack is getting tall. On the bottom is the letter from Lisa's lawyers. It's been sitting there for a week now. Or maybe it's been months. I don't know. I don't want to know. It can't be good news. Good news comes from Lisa in a manic phone call. She's reconsidered. She wants to talk. She's drunk. She's horny. She's forgiving. I love good news. Bad news comes from her lawyers. Bad news usually leads to more bad news.

I'm not opening that letter.

I have fantasies about disemboweling her lawyers. Cutting them open and removing their intestines so they can see them. Holding them up in the daylight should they care to take a look as they die a slow, painful, aware death. They're bad people who enjoy their jobs on top of it. I'd use the dullest knife I could find.

I am the sticky, syrupy, sinful residue of a hate reduction sauce. I am thick. I am obstinate in my despair. I am nothing. I'm not opening that letter.

But I should pay those bills. Maybe I'll send the letter to the power company. They can deal with it.

An hour later, I'm sitting behind my desk listening to some douchebag whine about an inheritance. His grandfather left him a nice cut of the bazillion dollars he earned as a captain of some industry and I can tell already that if this asswipe has his way he'll burn through it before he's thirty. He's twenty-eight.

Lucky for him, there's no chance of that. No, he'll live a safe, padded life thanks to the strict discipline his great-grandfather laid down on his grandfather that leads to the kind of strength and willpower and lack of scruples that results in fortunes this large. On the other hand, it also leads to a lifestyle that produces offspring who don't know their fathers or, in turn, how to father. So what you end up with is a lot of money and a fuckwad grandson who seems to think he's entitled to the keys to the bank.

Instead, what Junior here gets is a structured payout that's tiered to different ages tied, in theory, to corresponding leaps in personal growth and responsibility. He got a hundred grand as soon as the old man dropped dead. Basically a bonus for showing up at the funeral. At thirty, he gets another five hundred, the assumption being that he will be in the mood to marry around then and this will pay for the wedding and eliminate any of the speed bumps so many newlyweds and poor married people have with regard to money. At forty, he gets a check for another million, to make sure Douchey McDouche's kids are taken care of. At fifty, he gets the rest. Three million. What was that geezer thinking? I tried to steer him toward donating it to charity or leaving it to a beloved cat, but he wouldn't have any of it. He had a soft spot for the boy and from what I could tell, felt that he had failed his own son by not being around while earning all the god damn money. So this was a make-good. Not that it would make anything good. The kid was lost a long time ago.

He's wheedling around trying to convince me that he's so smart he can handle all this financial stuff himself. Never mind the weeks I spent sitting with the guy who actually made the money ensuring everything was just so for little mister man here. I'm waiting for him to start questioning our rate and asking for a retroactive break on the price his old man already paid. Like we give refunds. Meanwhile, he's wearing a brand new Cartier Pasha. Yesterday, it was an Ernst Benz ChronoScope. Sorry all that free money isn't enough for you, Hoss. Nice to see you're making smart decisions before the check even clears.

I think I punched a garbage man last night. Or a bum. One of the two was breaking my balls about not being able to stand up. My knuckles are all scratched up so that must have been it. Or I fell. But usually falling means scratches on my palms and face. Must have been a punch.

There's no way to hide the scabs since we're going over the details in these documents and I have to keep pointing things out to this dumbass. I don't care. Not a little.

To each of his idiotic questions I nod and shrug and recite the lines that service my client while protecting the firm. Twelve years sitting in this chair. The wheedling pansy in front of me doesn't have any new problems. And I hate his tie. I wonder if he's ever been hit in the face. Probably not, but I'm telling you it would do him some good.

Once I get rid of him there are a few other clients and meetings and some conference calls to attend to. They all go pretty much the same. I get through them playing a tepid version of my former self. Thank god I'm a meaningless cog in this vapid machine. I could be replaced in a matter of hours if anyone cared to make the effort. So far no one has. I wonder how long this can last. Not much longer. I am a victim of inertia. When I was on my way up, I couldn't be stopped. I had three job offers the second I passed the bar. I doubled my salary twice in seven years thanks to some brash self-marketing and shrewd interview choices. I quickly became the darling of my current firm's founder, sitting in with his biggest clients and gaining experience my peers wouldn't come close to until they had put in another decade of grunt work and ass kissing.

I was being groomed for bigger things.

Whispers of making me a partner had even begun circulating for a brief second or two. How I must have been hated. But that was when I was on my way up. I am now on my way down and it would appear that once again nothing can stop me.

My head is pounding and there's only so much coffee I can drink before the balance tips from beneficial by way of caffeine buzz and energy boost to an annoying incessant need to urinate causing me to excuse myself three or four times from the same meeting. Unprofessional.

I wish I had some coke. I don't. I have to gut it out.

My debit card is missing. I'm guessing it's at a bar, but fuck me if I know which one. I should cancel it, but I don't. I will. Just not now. It would take seventy-two seconds to cancel it and order a new one. It's exhausting to even think about.

I spend the conference calls grunting agreement with whatever is being said and drawing detailed vignettes of my clients in sexual positions they may or may not enjoy in real life. The fat banker with the twitchy eye swallows a cock where I should be writing down interest rates or fees or something important. An old lady I've never met gets a Penthouse body and Jessica Rabbit tits and a Mandingo boyfriend putting the stones to her from behind. I forgot how much artistic talent I've been ignoring my adult life. Too late now to do anything serious with it. Maybe I'll start an anonymous Tumblr with these and see if they go viral. They won't. I won't.

Hours later, my headache is dissipating. I think of myself as heroic in my struggle against the lingering damage of the night before. I'm a gladiator. I am the myth behind the man. I can't wait to go to sleep.

Lisa doesn't call. I check my cell to see if I drunk dialed or texted her last night. Nope. Between meetings I try her office. Nothing. I hang up before the voicemail picks up. Her office phone has caller ID.

The final meeting of the day includes my direct supervisor and former mentor, Harry. I haven't seen a lot of him lately. His choice. We've had our talks and he's suggested things like taking some time off or maybe not putting myself under so much stress. What is unspoken but understood is that I've disappointed him both as a lawyer and a man.

The meeting is brutal because it involves me discussing numbers and details and I have to pay attention even though I want to put my eyes out with a staple gun to stop looking at these papers that I hate so much.

I run the meeting and Harry sits like a granite lion at the end of the table. Harry's gravitas alone is worth an extra hundred grand in billing from this client. He's a big, navy, pin-striped security blanket. He's watching me closely. If I'm getting anything wrong, he isn't correcting me. I think things are going well. Considering.

I wrap the meeting up, our clients sign some papers and hands are shaken. Another satisfied customer gets fed a few bad jokes, has their back patted, and is escorted to the elevator. I know this was a test. I know I failed. Inertia.

Harry watches the doors close and turns to me, staring me down as only a disgusted father figure can.

—Everything okay?

—No. Why?

—Because you've been acting like an ass and you look like shit.

—I'm fine. I'll be fine.

Harry looks me over. I can't tell if he's going to fire me or hug me or is just thinking about what he's going to have for dinner.

—Christian. We've talked about this. Enough. Get your act together.

Harry walks away, a flaccid smile on his face for the receptionist who may or may not have heard our conversation.

7

(Oh, the perils of divorce.)

As our man at the bar can tell you, should you muster the courage to engage him—but, again, I urge you please do not—the path of separation is fraught with ugly pain and selective memory and endless meditation on impossible alternate realities.

What if we had met later in life?

What if we had tried counseling earlier?

What if I was a person of stronger character?

Yes, the contemplative possibilities are rich and fascinating and, although ultimately fruitless, have armed the old boy with plenty to ponder as he pours himself into another extended evening of overpriced spirits and impulsive aggression.

Tonight's activities take place at a venue similar to our last encounter, only slightly lower toned. This is not to say our man's taste is faltering. He is simply changing things up. Adding a bit of variety to this long, slow drift into nothingness.

Look around and you'll see a class of people who are more than comfortable paying good money to be seen here. Further, the customers in attendance, for the most part, did not attain their social or economic position as a matter of accident or coincidence. At least half of every couple here is a person of ambition and determination, and to some degree, obstinance. And so, as the evening's shenanigans begin, the response to the old boy's behavior is not unpredictable or surprising in the slightest.

—Another one.

—Grey Goose martini, olives, up. Yes, sir.

If you're the nosy type, you've already observed and noted the four spent olive skewers lined up in front of our man's almost empty glass. Not unlike the skulls certain primitive tribes will post on spears outside their village as a warning to potential trespassers. You've more than likely also calculated his upcoming drink to be the fifth of this very early evening.

The martini is produced in record time and served up with the same precious showmanship as the previous masterpieces.

—My shift is ending, so if you wouldn't mind, I'll run your tab and start a new one for my replacement.

Our man waves his hand to indicate that this is a nonissue. He is hitting his stride and shan't be concerned with such trivialities as money or manners. His posture is foreboding. His breath is a weapon. His demeanor is a charismatic malignance. He scans the room for new arrivals.

Oh, my. There, a few seats down, in the black dress. You probably saw her come in, but our man was too busy with his own myopic reflections to notice until now. He quietly inventories her various physical attributes. She's attractive, but on the far side of thirty. She's confident enough to sit at a bar alone but her cosmetic enhancements do signal a need for attention. Her potential for illicit entertainment is intoxicating. His predator eyes narrow as his reptilian brain assumes command, superseding whatever discretion may have lingered from the few hours he spends sober these days.

In his perfect world, our man would sweep this temptress off her feet, shower her with effortless conversation, witty compliments, and his own personal brand of winning charm. The poor girl would swoon and her heart would race and she would fall truly, madly, deeply in love with him. She would beg him to be hers forever, to never leave, and to promise his everlasting devotion. She would give herself to him fully and completely. She would sacrifice her dreams and relinquish her ambitions.

She would forsake her family and friends to slavishly worship at the altar of their romance. She would be his.

In this fantasy world, our man would wait for that particular moment wherein the transformation from stranger to lover was complete, look deep into her eyes, savoring her unwavering vulnerability, the purity of the moment. And then he would crush her dreams and break her spirit and ruin her for all other men. Grinding her into the powdered version of the fiercely independent woman she once was. He would complete the act by walking away without explanation or hope for reconciliation, perhaps chuckling to himself about how easy the task had been. Some women never learn.

But you know as well as I that our man hasn't the immediate enterprise or long-term resolve required of an endeavor of such scope. He enjoys the fantasy, though. A satisfying scratch to the itch that has of late been a constant in the back of his angry little mind.

As the old boy weighs the likelihood of success of the various options of approach available to him, he is interrupted by the thoughtless bartender.

—I'm sorry, sir, but your card was rejected. I ran it three times.

Well, that certainly puts a damper on whatever strategy was bubbling up in our man's consciousness, no? Or perhaps it serves to catalyze tonight's inevitable meltdown. One might even picture the old boy grateful for the unexpected surplus of fuel that his self-loathing psychological apparatus burns at such a high rate. Hurrah!

Our man takes his card back and carelessly drops five twenty-dollar bills on the bar. Small embarrassments like this are best left in the past as soon as possible.

—Keep it.

—Thank you, sir.

Our man sips his drink and returns his attention to the unavoidably beautiful woman in the black dress.

—Can I buy you a drink?

—Doesn't sound like it.

To be fair to the old boy and his growing rage, she makes no effort to look over when responding. Clearly a move calculated to intensify the humiliation our man is now enjoying. He was attempting to move on from the shame, for God's sake. And to top things off, she raises the drink she already has with a hand that bears the diamond wedding ring on which some lucky fellow apparently spent a great deal of money. The nerve!

As far as our man is concerned, she has done the heavy lifting for him. He has been unequivocally forced into the corner he so desperately wants to be in. He affects a tolerant smile, fishes another twenty-dollar bill (his last) out of his wallet and slides it slowly in her direction, savoring the drama microsecond by microsecond.

—Well then. How about a blow job?

Ho ho! Now he has the whole of her wide-eyed attention. She even turns slightly to face him—an added bonus for the old boy as she's allowing a better view of her prominently displayed décolletage.

It is unclear whether the brief silence that follows our man's inquiry is due to her being stunned speechless or her gathering her thoughts before launching a concise but vicious riposte. We shall never know.

The gentleman with whom she arrived when our man did not see her enter now approaches, sliding a smooth, territorial hand across the small of his bride's back.

—Our table is ready.

—This guy called me a hooker.

Her significant other bristles as blood rushes from his brain to his muscles.

—Excuse me?

Upon further inspection, you'll notice the lady's escort is a man of great physical stature, naturally thick and exercised on top of that. A brute. Watch as he presents a posture of alpha male, leaning in toward the drunk who is noticeably thirty pounds lighter and five years older. Our man's face falls into the easy smile of inevitability.

—Sorry.

The old boy lets his apology linger as he sips what he knows will be his last drink in this bar. And by sip, obviously, I mean gulp. Despite his gag reflex flaring in response to the sudden harsh intake of vodka, he gallantly presses on, delivering his final word on the subject.

—Easy mistake with that perfume.

Well, the husband's meaty fist striking the center of our man's face is no surprise to any of us. What is worth noting is the ease with which our man absorbs the blow. He flies backward, taking a few of the beautiful but uncomfortable bar stools with him. Nearby waiters swarm the combatants and the manager chirps for them to be expelled and the crowd watches the most exciting thing that will happen in their presence tonight. For them it is shocking.

Neither fighter resists as they are escorted quickly through the front door of the establishment. In the case of our man, this is all going as planned. As to the muscular gentleman, there is the matter of defending his wife's honor—in his mind, a state of affairs far from settled.

Outside the restaurant, our man, there on the sidewalk, holds his hand to his nose. Not to stop the bleeding—an impossible task at this point—but to feel his own blood racing out of him. To know that he has accomplished something. A few more punches to his face and a final kick in the gut leave the old boy a soiled mess on the pavement. The husband of the lady in the black dress finishes the job by spitting on the side of our man's face as he lies there motionless. The old boy manages to cough out a loosened crown and some of the blood that clogs his throat. It is the one act he has managed tonight that is not contrived for attention.

The most delicate hint of a smile crosses his face as he fades to black and we take our leave, the work of the evening finished.

8

It's one of those perfect summer evenings.

A man I met less than five minutes ago is punching me in the face. His form is magnificent. This guy has put in some time at the gym. I wonder if he ever fought Golden Gloves or anything organized. He definitely should have. Pretty sure my nose is broken.

I'm wondering why things never work out for me. Why I never get the lucky breaks. What could I have done differently in my life? What other choices could I have made? What other paths could I have taken? Could I have been a different person or is this who I was always destined to be? What could have been?

This is my time to think. Me time.

The guy is breathing heavy from the exertion of bitch slapping me. He says some sort of Clint Eastwood tough guy thing to me but I'm not paying attention and don't want to be distracted from my internal monologue.

Why has my life taken the turns it has? Why (aside from my obvious breach of etiquette) is this guy on top while I'm on the bottom? Why has the universe decided that I should be a loser? I'm not talking about the ass whipping I'm enduring right now. That I'm grateful for. I mean in general. Big picture. Taken as a whole, I'm not thrilled with my life. I didn't ask for it to end up this way. I tried to avoid a lot of it but I never got the breaks. Why are some people lucky while some aren't?

I mean, look at this guy's hair. It's perfect. He's got an amazing hairline even in what must be his early thirties. Not an iota of recession.

And he's tall. Wonder if he talks to his parents on a regular basis. Probably has a healthy savings account. Investments. I bet his kids are handsome. His son will probably lose his virginity before he's sixteen and not knock up any of the dumbshits who fuck him in high school. I bet this guy started a business on his own and sells something that makes him money and he doesn't have to answer to a boss or sit through meetings he didn't call. I bet his employees treat him like they like him and only motherfuck him a little when he's not around. I bet his wife still thinks he's cute and they've been married for seven years already. I bet she thinks he's interesting and a good provider and a great father and they talk and share and enjoy each other's company. I think she's looking at him right now like she's a little turned on. It's hard to tell with the blood in my eyes. Lucky guy.

I could be wrong about all this, but I don't think I am. This guy has it better than me. Why is that?

It helps for me to clear my head sometimes. Take a moment and try to figure it all out.

This is my meditation.

It occurs to me (as he winds up for what I assume, judging by my fading consciousness, will be his final blow) that the most difficult and critical parts of a marriage are composed of the most forgettable interactions. It's not the grandiose wedding ceremony or getting the right dinner reservations for Valentine's Day or buying her the emerald necklace for your third anniversary that's important. It's smiling when you pass each other at home on a quiet Sunday. Or remembering that she likes a little extra basil in her pasta sauce. Or offering to drive because she doesn't like the highways and it's not that big of a fucking deal for me to do it. That's what makes a marriage strong and long-lasting.

Now I realize. This is my epiphany.

No way this guy knows that. No way he's intellectualized it, analyzed it, wrapped it up in a nice, neat package like I have. But I figured it out. It just took a little thinking when this fucktard is hammering me with his bitch wife getting wet in the background. I bet he never figures it out.

Who's lucky now, asshole?

9

*It's three and a half years ago.

I've been dating Lisa on and off again for six months.

I won't say it's against my will, but I'll say it's close.

I'm sitting across the table from her at our third-favorite restaurant. No way I should have the glass of wine I'm ordering but that was also true for the glasses before it and the one I'll have after it, so fuck it. I'm watching her face and thinking she's so beautiful when she smiles and thank god I found her and I'm waiting for her to say the wrong thing so I can pounce on it with some passive-aggressive bullshit because that's what we do. You have to enjoy the good stuff while it's there.

—Another Shiraz, please.

The overly attentive waitress makes sure I know she approves of my selection before padding off to leave Lisa and me back in our own little romantic world.

Dating isn't the right word. I feel that's a little formal for what we've been up to. This thing we have is more visceral. Feral. What do you call it when mountain lions get together? Are they the ones that mate and then the female eats the male? I might be thinking of the praying mantis. But Lisa moves more like a mountain lion.

My stupid ex-girlfriend, Dana, brought Lisa around a couple more times after our first inadvertent meeting. She never asked if she could, they just showed up as a twosome. So I kind of blame Dana. Once she even dragged Lisa to a dinner at my apartment that was supposed to be a congratulatory affair for a friend who landed a big job. The friend was neither my stupid ex-girlfriend nor Lisa so I'm not sure why I invited Dana or why she decided that it was so important to bring her uninvited plus-one. Maybe Dana was trying to set us up. No. She's not that smart. I knew she would bring Lisa.

Our mutual distaste was palpable, although both of us liked to confuse it for sparks or chemistry or whatever makes you grab someone at the end of the night and grin conspiratorially and kiss them passionately and tell yourself four hours later that you're a god damned idiot and what the fuck were you thinking? But then it's too late and all you can do is continue to sop up the vomit you're cleaning off the floor and hope you can fake sleep well enough in the morning that she'll take off without saying goodbye.

I invited Dana to a few more events anticipating that she would bring Lisa. She did and we sharpened our claws on each other again and again. Easy to recognize as foreplay in hindsight, every evening ending with drunken mashing, and by the third or fourth time we wound up in her bed. Or I should say we woke up in her bed. I honestly couldn't remember if we had sex that night or not. We didn't talk about it until months later when she told me we did, but only until I passed out.

Two months of that before we throw in the towel and tell the supporting characters in our dating lives that they're out and we dive in to whatever the relationship was back then.

Sparring. That's the word for what we're doing now. Sparring like kung fu practice partners. Drawn to each other by that magic that attracts people like us to the lovers who are the absolute worst for them. A thirst for adventure. Self-loathing. Masochism.

It would appear that love can be forged out of virtually anything, no matter how toxic.

We dine and drink and fuck and fight and ignore every single red flag and this similarly charged magnet inserts herself into my core and I know I won't be able to live without her no matter what she does to me. She takes a little piece of me and tells me it matters to her and she is going to keep it and there is nothing I can do about it. I let her.

My Shiraz comes or maybe it doesn't. We're leaving the restaurant, staggering only a little and I'm making her giggle which feels good. She laughs at my jokes most of the time now and when she does she makes it a point to look me in the eye like I've done something special that only we know about. A secret language I can barely translate.

She's leaning on me and holding my arm at the elbow with both hands. She's finishing her story about her first job out of college promoting eyeglass frames and making way too much money for a twenty-three-year-old and I realize that I'm probably going to ask her to marry me in the very near future and I'm wondering if I'm not making a huge mistake and I decide that it doesn't matter or it does and I forget and we walk out to go to a martini bar I read about.

Sparring. Like two old barflies who can take a punch and like it.

10

I'm at the office on time as usual, but creaky with bruises from my night out on top of the cumulative effects of my mini-bender. The animatronic receptionist on the nineteenth floor makes sure to both catch my eye and ignore the bruising around it. Her skin is amazing.

—Mr. Hunter would like to see you first thing.

Couldn't even let me get settled in my fucking office, huh? Barely even through my second venti latte and Harry wants to have a heart-to-heart. Not entirely surprising since I gave his name as my emergency contact last night. Why was that again? To show Lisa I didn't give a shit about her anymore? The logic made sense at the time. So did the decision to walk out of the hospital and grab a cab before Harry got there. The evening seems to have been a series of bad choices. But, fuck it. I jingle what's left of the Valium I stole from the ER nurse around in my pocket and mull over popping one more before I get to Harry's.

—Sorry about last night. I wasn't, uh, thinking straight.

Harry stands at the floor to ceiling window soaking in his formidable view of lower Manhattan. That would be me in twenty years if I chose to get my shit together. Looking out my fat ass windows thinking about what I could have done with my life if I weren't a lawyer. I hate Harry, but only for a second.

I sit in one of the plush chairs and brace myself for another beating. An unexpected bonus.

He says nothing, which is typical. I know he's weighing several tacks of approach and I wish he would settle on one so we could move forward and he can yell at me and I can nod and apologize. I have the phrases 'rough patch' and 'bear with me' locked and loaded and may refer to him as my 'rock' if I see an opening. When this is over I'll go sleep at my desk. How much can he take, I wonder? How much leeway is twelve years of eighty- to one-hundred-hour weeks worth? Probably not much.

—Is this still about Lisa? You know you're not the first guy to go through this.

He's going to go easy on me. Jesus, Harry. You pussy.

I don't answer. He'll think that means something significant. It doesn't. Harry turns to face me.

—Enough. I thought you were getting help.

—I had a few drinks. That's it. Again, I'm sorry.

—When was the last time you saw Dr. Hirsch?

I've never seen Dr. Hirsch. Hirsch doesn't exist. I made him up to get Harry to stop bothering me about getting professional help. It doesn't matter how I answer this question so, again, I don't.

—The drinking. The bar fights. The bizarre behavior. Look at your face, for the love of Christ. Who knows what else you're up to that I don't even hear about.

—Harry, I'm having some problems. A rough patch. This is tough. You've been there. But it's not affecting my work. I'm still the best player on your team.

All morning I swore to myself that I would take it easy tonight. Maybe watch a movie. Read. One glass of wine, tops. Probably nothing. Stay dry. It's twelve hours until morning. Ten if I kill some time at the gym. Staying late and catching up on work would help. I thought that was a good plan ten minutes ago. Now I'm thinking tequila. My head feels loose and I need to tighten it up.

—Adam Galen asked you off his business this morning.

Oh he did, did he? The son of a bitch.

Definitely tequila. I can taste the crackle of a generous double shot hitting the back of my throat, irritating and soothing at the same time. That's how you start off an evening. My mouth starts to water a little.

—Look, I'll deal with it.

—Yes. You will.

Harry hands me an appointment card for a psychiatrist who claims to be named Dr. Arnold Rosen. I have a sinking feeling he is a real person.

Oh Harry, if you only knew what a bad idea this is. Now is not the time to explain to him what I would politely call my aversion to therapy. He's not in the mood. But we seem to have come to a bit of an impasse here. The unstoppable force meeting the drunken, self-destructive, hopeless object. I wonder if I ran full speed could I break through the window behind Harry. Doubtful.

Handwritten on the front of the card: *Tuesday, 2:30 P.M.*

You've got to be kidding me. What an ambush. I need time to think. Time to make excuses. To leave town.

—What, like today Tuesday?

—Like today Tuesday. Go.

If my brain weren't completely flat in my head, I could maybe possibly talk my way out of this. But right now all I can come up with are caveman grunts and fist clenching motions. Probably not appropriate.

—Christian, it's completely confidential. Not even going on the company's insurance. I'm picking this up personally. I know this guy. He's good. Helped me when I went through my troubles. Besides, I'm not asking. I'm telling.

—I don't need this.

—You need something. Go. It might help.

It might. But I doubt it.

11

This is my earliest memory.

I'm nine.

I'm sitting in the office of the hack that Foster Mother makes me go to once a week. It's court ordered but she doesn't have to follow it to the letter, right? Who would know if I didn't show up and she didn't tell anyone? No one. The hack doesn't care. He works for the state and the void I would leave in his schedule would get filled instantly with some other sad sack shithead. I wouldn't be a blip in his rearview mirror.

But she makes me go. I think she has a good heart. Or she's scared. Maybe she needs to get out of the house. Either way, she's not my real mother and I hate being here.

I'm nine and even I know this guy is a low-rent hack. His suit is ugly and his shoes are cheap and his office smells like the shitty cigars he smokes between court-mandated sessions. His carpet is shag and I wonder when was the last time it was cleaned. My best guess is never. It lies there listening to all the shit his patients dump and it soaks it all up and no one ever cleans it. Shit soaked shag.

I have other memories of lying awake in bed and playing basketball with my friends after school and the first time I saw Foster Mother naked. But this is the earliest one.

I'm sitting on the far end of the couch. Jammed up against the armrest. As if that will help. The wood under the barely there padding digs into my ribs but I don't do anything about it. Dr. HackShag sits across the room waiting patiently for me to tell him about my week and how I've been coping with the loss of my mother. He wants to know if the nightmares have continued. I mean it's only been three weeks. What does he expect? I'm nine and I know the nightmares will never stop.

The good news is that I never remember what these horrible dreams are about. I understand on a visceral level what their subject matter is, but I don't recall the actual narrative once I wake up screaming. It all dissolves into aftertaste like a thin breath mint.

It must be very frustrating for Foster Mother. She's the one who has to deal with it every god damned night. Foster Father sleeps through all the yelling. Couldn't give a shit anyway. I think Foster Mother secretly enjoys it. Taking care of me and Ella gives her life purpose. What else is she doing? Opening beers for her pot-bellied husband and cashing our checks? I give her a reason to live. Also my nightmares become fodder for gossip with her faux-horrified friends. You're welcome.

I don't remember my first day of school or being toilet trained or my eighth birthday party which I may or may not have had. But I remember this. I'm nine and I'm sitting in the hack's office staring at the disgusting shag under my feet. The carpet looks like it's slowly inhaling my shoes. Shag quicksand. I know struggling will only make it worse and then I'll never get out. I remember knowing what happened to my mother.

I remember understanding that my father killed my mother in the most brutal fashion knowing full well I was watching. He was that kind of guy. I don't remember the event itself or being remanded into the foster care system. But I remember being aware that it all happened as I sat in that musty office. It's my earliest memory.

This is six months before Dr. HackShag rapes me during one of our sessions. We wade through half a year of mediocre therapy before he gets to the point. The brilliance of the whole thing is the groundwork he lays before he tells me he wants to try something different and to shut my fucking mouth when I start crying and struggling. Months of telling Foster Mother that I'm a compulsive liar who needs lots of help. Months of planning for two minutes of sloppy domination. Brilliant. If this kind of stuff is important to you.

This is six months before I throw away my blood soaked underwear and say nothing for weeks. Six months before I don't know what I feel more of—shame or loneliness.

After the rape, Dr. HackShag acts as if nothing out of the ordinary happened. The session after he shoved his runty cock up my clenched ass he asks how my week was. I tell him it was fine and we spend the rest of the court-ordered fifty minutes trying some lame hypnosis that's doomed from the start because fuck if I'm going to close my eyes ever again with that guy in the room.

When I finally tell Foster Mother something terrible happened, she nods and says she understands but I have to find a way to deal with stress besides telling stories about people who are trying to help me. We got to the next session fifteen minutes early.

I'm nine. This is my first memory.

12

Lisa begged me to go to counseling. At first, anyway. For myself. For us. I flat out refused individual therapy with no explanation. I was taking my boyhood therapy adventure to the grave with me. Sorry, nonnegotiable.

I know she meant well but there were bigger issues at hand. Lately though, I wonder what if I had gone? What if I had sucked it up and seen someone? For Lisa. What if I had opened up even the tiniest bit to a stranger with a psychology degree? Could it really have been that bad? Talking to a therapist was nothing but air coming out of my mouth. It's not like I couldn't walk out of the session if so much as the guy's tie offended me. At worst, I talk for an hour and never go back. And what if they had something insightful to say? What if I took them seriously and did the work I needed to do? What if I was fixable? The world might be a very different place. Too late now.

What-ifs aside, I didn't want the crutch, personally or as a couple. I didn't understand why we couldn't work things out ourselves. We had managed to find each other despite overwhelming odds. We fell in love. We made a life together. So why bring a stranger in to sort things out? It would never work. How could they possibly understand the intricacies of our relationship? We're unique. I don't care how many couples Dr. Smartypants had counseled before. We deserved special treatment and I knew we wouldn't get it. There would be shortcuts.

Oh, I've seen this before.

I know where this is going.

This is exactly like the Rosenbergs from last year.

And even if we managed to find the one super-talented counselor who could appreciate our bond for what it was, they would inevitably side with one of us or the other. That's how people work.

If they side with Lisa, I play the persecuted victim and nothing gets done. If they side with me, I feel like a bully and overcompensate by taking the blame for everything and then resent both of them for putting me in that position. I knew how it would go down. Without a doubt. I knew it would be lose/lose. But I agreed anyway.

Lisa let the individual therapy slide when I said I'd think about the couples version. I can still see the look on her face when I told her. Shock isn't the word. It's not powerful enough. I could be unreasonable and she knew my agreement was a big compromise. Lisa was nothing if not practical. I don't know why I caved so easily. Maybe to get my personal stuff off the table as soon as possible. Yeah, that was it. I was terrified.

As soon as I agreed, her mood lightened noticeably. As if the problem were solved already. As if she were happy after so many months. It was a dramatic enough turnaround that I wondered if the real point all along was to see if she could get me to go to therapy. The therapy itself more of an afterthought. Gravy.

She had the name of a doctor who had worked wonders for Michelle and her husband and would be perfect for us. Fucking Michelle. The doctor was a woman. Michelle's husband was a broken man. I couldn't stand him almost as much as I couldn't stand Michelle. I procrastinated and postponed committing to an appointment for months and finally everything else boiled over and overwhelmed us and Lisa stopped asking. We both knew things had become more than what Michelle's miracle doctor could handle.

And here I was again with a new mandate to see a counselor. I'm aware there are worse recurring patterns to have in one's life, but I don't love this one. I'm going through with it because I am under the impression that I should keep my job. I just can't think of why that is so god damned important anymore. How much of this is rote repetition of what is understood to be an acceptable American life I don't know. Lately, when I'm not out of control, I'm on autopilot.

I'm sure he'll smell booze on me should I care to indulge before our session so I don't. The inside of my head is already starting to tingle. Dying for a scotch. I told Harry I'd come. A yes for Harry and a no for Lisa.

Sorry, Lisa.

Fuck you, Harry.

I don't care what comes out of today. Arnold Rosen will never fix me. He doesn't have the tools and Harry doesn't have enough money. That makes this oh so much easier to swallow. Also I plan on saying nothing or lying when I do speak.

Lying. Lying. Lying.

Rosen sits there with his beard and his glasses and his five feet, eight inches of bald headed, soft-peddled authority. Waiting. How do they make psychiatrists' offices so god damn quiet anyway?

—Would it be easier for you to address me as Arnold?

—Is that what the rest of your patients do?

—Depends. Christian, I understand your first session can be awkward. Especially if you've never been in therapy before. So let's make it as easy as possible. We'll treat this like a first date and get used to each other's faces.

There's no way for Arnold Rosen, M.D. to know this but a reference to dating from a therapist I'm being forced to see is not a great start to our relationship. At least he's got nice shoes. And oriental rugs on wood floors. I told him I've never been in therapy before so he thinks this is virgin territory for me. Fuck him. Let him earn it.

—Before we get started, do you have anything you want to talk about? Anything on your mind?

My wife left me. I hate my job. My boss is about to fire me. I drink too much. I've wasted my life. I pick fights with perfect strangers. I'm worthless. If I disappeared no one would notice. I lack the capacity to feel joy. I'm thirty-eight and I miss the parents I never really knew. Hmm, how do I sum this up?

—Nope.

—Do you have any questions for me? About me? My credentials?

—No. You came highly recommended.

—Ah, yes. Well, I don't think I'm breaking any confidences when I tell you that Harry is very concerned about what he believes is self-destructive behavior on your part. Would you like to discuss that?

—I drink a little sometimes. To relieve stress.

I avoid the eyes of the doctor who flosses every day and pays his taxes and probably fucking tithes.

—So, Christian, where are you from?

—Brooklyn. Bay Ridge. Born and raised.

—No accent.

—Not anymore.

—Where did you go to school?

—Brooklyn College. NYU Law.

Dr. Rosen moves his forehead to affect a barely perceptible nod as he takes a moment to absorb this information and, I assume, to judge my educational background in comparison to his, the ever-so-noticeable Ivy League degrees hanging on his wall.

—Married?

—Not anymore.

He makes a note in his pretentious, leather-bound, legal pad binder.

—Kids?

—No.

—When did you first try to kill yourself?

Oh, this motherfucker.

Got to be a lucky guess, right? No way he can read me that well after ten minutes of chit chat. He can't be that good. I hate that his beard makes him look understanding. I know he's dying to hear the answer. And the fucking bravado of jumping in like that with a big bold question and no ramp up. He's showing off. Flexing his muscles. Dominating. Probably has a hard on.

—Why would I try to kill myself?

Dr. Rosen waits for an answer. How much money did those types of pretentious silences cost his patients? What a rip off.

His face is tranquil. A perfectly bland mix of curiosity and patience. I know he's not going to say another word until I answer. And he'll rat me out if I don't. I wonder if he's taping this for Harry. Fucking hate this guy.

—High school.

Lying. Lying. Lying.

—And?

—And it was pathetic. I didn't even come close. Got it totally wrong.

I pull my sleeve up to reveal a beauty of a faded scar across my wrist. I indicate the proper direction one needs to slice to get the job done correctly. Down. You have to slice vertical, dummy.

—Can't walk across. Gotta run down.

My almost-suicide was dismissed by Foster Father as a weak play for attention. It wasn't. Foster Mother didn't know what to think. She kept asking me if I was gay.

They never found the note I left on my dresser. I really didn't plan it out very well. Left the bathroom door unlocked. Didn't wait for them to leave the house. What a dope. I bled for maybe five minutes before Foster Mother came in to put some towels away. I didn't even get sleepy.

—Why'd you do it?

—Don't remember. Depressed. Dumb.

—And since then?

Since then, two more none-of-your-G-D-business times in the same year. Plus, I'm lying about my first time anyway. If we're really being honest, we should count the time I tried to walk in front of a bus three months before I cut my wrists. But let the good doctor prove it. Fat chance.

—Nothing. I'm fine.

Dr. Rosen makes a few smug notes in the file on his lap. I wonder if he'll have a good laugh about this with his moderately attractive wife over their low-carb dinner tonight. My head is starting to throb.

—Let's talk about family. Your dad.

Arnold Rosen, you don't have enough time left in your self-satisfied life to listen to me discuss my father. You don't have the brain power to absorb the complexities of my relationship with that monster. You don't have the empathetic capacities to relate to the turmoil I felt after that night until, well, now. I was there and I don't get it.

To be honest, it's kind of amusing to see you approach the subject. As if you had the chops to climb this wall. Do you know how many people have tried? My friends tried to do it and I liked them. My wife couldn't do it and I was crazy about her. But you, I don't like. No, not at all. So good eff-ing luck.

—What about him?

—Nice guy?

—Sure.

—Your mom?

—She died when I was eight.

—How?

If only to see the look on your face. And to make sure you tell Harry I was forthcoming on some level. Here's a tasty little morsel for you, Arnold Rosen. I hope you choke on it.

—My father shot her in the face while she was reading me a bedtime story.

God dammit, Arnold. How dare you sit there and not react. How dare you narrow your eyes and try to move the conversation forward. Like you're interested.

—I thought you said he was a nice guy.

—Relatively speaking.

I've got a headache like someone poured hot sauce on the back of my eyeballs. Why won't this guy leave me alone? I know it's his job, but Jesus.

—Tell me about your parents. Before your mom died.

—I don't remember anything before that.

—What does that mean?

I hate you, Arnold Rosen. You presumptuous bastard. Sitting there acting like you care. What if you weren't getting paid? What then? How much would you want to know the details? How much would you knit those big, bushy eyebrows and pretend to focus on me and my issues?

Not much. I'm quite sure something pressing would come up. Or would you have me stay here anyway and finish my thought? What if we were fifteen sessions into it and the financial plug got pulled? Would you be okay with telling me to piss off then? I bet you would. I bet my seat wouldn't be cold before it was filled with some other idiot dying to tell you about their uncle touching them or their husband ignoring them or whatever secrets might take up those fifty minutes of your overpriced day. You're a whore, Arnold Rosen. Just like the rest of us.

—I don't remember anything before the age of nine.

—Nothing?

No, nothing. Oh, and no one ever bothered to address it. Not really. To answer a few of your other obvious questions, Arnold—Yes, I told my first therapist about it. He did nothing; Yes, I told Foster Mother about it. She told me to be patient; Yes, I told Lisa about it. That's when she started begging me to get therapy. In other words, she made it someone else's problem before I finished the sentence. I've been here before. Nothing is going to happen. I am empty. I am void. I am irreparable. But if you really need an answer, here's one.

—Apparently there's some trauma associated with seeing your mom killed by your father. PTSD-related memory repression. I hear.

—Well, we should discuss—

—I think our time is up.

My headache has become one of those freezing cold ice picks in the front of my brain. Talking is making it worse.

—No, we still have plenty of time.

At some point you have to know when to cut your losses. And since the doctor can't figure out that this conversation is going nowhere and I am fully aware that there are plenty of ways to screw your patients besides actually cornholing them, I decide to do us both a favor and end the session. Fuck Harry and fuck this guy and fuck Dr. HackShag and Foster Mother and everyone else.

I stand up and walk to the door. The doctor may or may not still be in the room. I no longer know or care. I have to leave.

—Christian, if I've struck a nerve, that might be a good thing. We should explore that.

Turns out the doctor is indeed still in the room and standing close enough to gently touch my arm. He actually thinks he might convince me to stay, the superior prick.

—Repressed memories can be some of the most powerful—

I grab the doctor by his somewhat expensive lapels and slam him against the wall. Our eyes meet and he looks scared.

Well, well, well, Arnold Rosen. Looks like we've entered into some unexplored territory on your side. Is that something you'd like to talk about? Are there any feelings you'd like to share with regards to this experience? Do you need a hug, Arnold?

I throw him across the room and he lands hard on his back. Good. He struggles to catch his breath like the pansy he is. I stand over him breathing hard as he holds the back of his head while he lays across a broken end table that must have taken some fag interior designer forever to find.

The red tint of rage recedes and I'm not sure where this is going. I'm confident I've made my point but I'm becoming unclear on what that point originally was.

13

*It's five weeks ago.

I'm at my desk alone, crying.

I don't know how I got here or how long I've been here. Reality is slowly coming back into focus. I am a lawyer. I work in an office. This office. This is my office. I appear to be upset about something. Anxious. My name is Christian. I take a deep breath and I'm pretty much back.

It's not the first time I've blacked out sober.

Last Thursday I woke up on a subway. The six train headed uptown. I was showered, shaved, and dressed for work. It was four in the afternoon and my fingertips were bleeding.

Four days before that I was in a restaurant. Suddenly awake, sitting at a table for two with a glass worth of cabernet dripping down my face. I don't know who threw it on me or why I was carrying a bottle of Xanax in my front pocket. I hate Xanax.

A week before that I woke up in a cab headed for the airport.

I'm in my office and I'm thinking about reconciliation and second chances and forgiveness because that's what people do. They make up. They forgive each other. They start over. Things can work out if you really want them to. Or if you will them to. If you make them. Everything is fixable.

I think that's what I'm thinking. It all evaporates so quickly when I wake up like this.

I want to call Lisa at her brother's house, but I know that's a terrible idea. Last time he told me I'd never speak to her again.

As if it's up to him.

What I should be doing is figuring out what I can say that would have any effect on her. A battle plan. A begging plan. Points of logic. A deal memo. A negotiating platform. Luck is the result of preparation and timing. I should be preparing.

I can't find a pen to save my life.

My assistant buzzes and asks if I'm ready for my two o'clock. I didn't realize it was after noon. Or daytime. I have no idea what I was just scrambling around for. I'm not wearing a tie. I tell my assistant I'm all set.

I don't bother wiping the tears from my eyes before my client enters. In retrospect, that may have been a mistake.

14

(Ahem.)

The evening is another smashing success.

Inspired by the honorable Dr. Arnold Rosen, our man plays by his gut and, with virtually no plan at all, manages to succeed in the generation of social entropy beyond even his wildest expectations.

The brassy statements of masculinity.

The purposeful overindulgence of alcohol.

The eager reception of so many well-placed blows.

They all work magnificently together in an elegant symphony of chaos and destruction. If things continue along this order, this may even be our man's swan song. His grand finale.

Tonight's adventure began with a lengthy bivouac at the bar of an establishment catering to a wilder crowd than our man is normally found in. Special prices for generic drinks. A dense hodgepodge of braying young men stacked mercilessly in a never-ending parade to and from the bar. A somewhat lacking representation of attractive, available women. Loud, violent music. The environment a virtual powder keg of machismo with a testosterone soaked fuse that was almost too easy to light. What is most surprising is not that our man has been beaten to utter stillness, it is that a member of the cheering audience took the time to call for medical assistance when the lopsided donnybrook was said and done.

Perhaps, the old boy thinks, at long last he will manage to make his point concretely understood by his ex-wife.

Meanwhile, the hard working emergency medical technicians in the back of the ambulance in which he is riding employ every neuron and muscle fiber available to them to keep our man alive. It's counterproductive to the old boy's agenda, but this is their sworn duty.

If you listen carefully you will hear them use phrases like 'blood pressure dropping' and 'can't find a pulse' to describe his quickly deteriorating condition. But they also mix in some pointed critiques of his lifestyle choices including 'What a waste,' 'Worse than I've ever seen,' and 'Idiot.' Inappropriate, but accurate.

The ambulance screams to a halt and the medics bark updates at the hospital staff as they scurry efficiently to save valuable seconds. Overhead, the ceiling lights pass over our man as if to create a countdown while his gurney and all attending personnel race from the emergency unloading deck to the awaiting emergency facilities. A gruesome parade in celebration of a feat of staggering dedication and heartbreaking majesty. According to the good people who rescued our man from the sidewalk where he lay alone outside the bar in which the altercation started, the old boy is an innocent victim of a random act of unprovoked violence. As far as they were able to determine. No one in the immediate vicinity claimed knowledge of how our man came to be in this condition and there was no time to track down cooperative eyewitnesses. The job at hand was to keep the old boy alive until arrival at the hospital and that was a herculean task even for the seasoned veterans.

The brilliant doctors inject our man with medicines and stimulants while constantly consulting and rechecking the very latest in technology to monitor his progress. They employ stopgap measures and quick fixes, thinking only in terms of the coming seconds. It's all they have.

Our man has a rather different view of the affair. He is elated, although his understanding of the details of what precisely is happening within his quickly failing mortal self is fuzzy and incomplete. He's a lawyer, not a doctor. But speaking from his general perspective of the evening's pugilistic activities, he is content with his performance and confident that he will defy the best efforts of these well-intentioned buffoons. Huzzah!

There will be no emergency contact to roust from deep slumber so early in the morning. The matter is settled and he relaxes whatever grip he had maintained on his mortal self. Ta da! He is on his way. Finished. Farewell. Bon Voyage.

If our man could have bowed, he would have.

15

White.

It's so white.

Wherever I am is so very white, white, white.

I may or may not be here. I have no sense of my body. Only my presence. I am everywhere and eternal and also right here condensed into nothing. It is only me.

And The White.

There is nothing to see but I know my vision is crystal clear. There is nothing to hear but I know I can perceive the smallest of sounds.

I have no thoughts beyond pure awareness. Finally. It feels so good. Enough of that other bullshit already. I should have done this a long time ago. The silence here is a thick bath of velvety emptiness that makes me feel clean and soft and even and I never want to leave. I'm breathing life in and out and if you were to touch me your troubles would disappear. I am not hopeful or repentant or anticipatory or nostalgic. I am emotional homeostasis. I'm perfect.

There is nothing around me. I know that the absence of any light creates black, but the presence of the entire spectrum of light creates white. So maybe there is everything around me.

The whoosh begins like a breath from a sleeping baby and grows quickly to the wail of a thousand mourning mothers. A tiny object appears on the horizon. It comes fast like the realization of bad news, racing toward me. When it hits me it is infinitely large. Unavoidable.

It's a memory.

A single memory pushing through me, reawakening neural connections I thought cauterized long ago.

It takes no time to pass through, but I can see everything it contains as it does.

I recognize my mother immediately. I saw pictures of her after she died. Does anyone ever think their mother is anything but beautiful? I remember nothing of her from my childhood but here, now, I see her and I know it's her and it feels so comfortable. This is real. 3D. She's right there. Moving. Breathing. Talking. With that thick black hair tied back and such a skinny waist. Pouring herself another glass of red wine. She is twenty-eight and I am five and there we are in our kitchen and she's making dinner. I even recognize the smell. She's tall or maybe that's my perception as a child. She moves like my sister. Always moving. Always cleaning or stirring something or mixing something. A restrained undercurrent of energy. Same eyes too. Same brown eyes. I bet Ella doesn't know that. The few pictures she could ever dig up were black and white newspaper reprints. I should tell her. I should tell Ella if I ever see her again.

—You want some juice, Christian?

Holy god, her voice. Completely new but familiar like it's a part of me. I want her to say more but my younger self only nods and she pours me a glass without another word. She's got a thick Brooklyn accent and when she looked at me I could see sweetness in her eyes. Such a pure moment and neither one of us noticed when it happened.

I'm coloring at the kitchen table, looking up every few seconds to make sure she's still there. I hear the neighbor wife bitching at her husband through our open window. It must be a regular thing because we don't react. The feeling in my five-year-old belly is contentment. It's a good day. I have no clue what's coming down the pike only a few years from now. My mother returns to making dinner. My god. She's gorgeous. My father walks in from outside and pulls a beer out of the refrigerator. Look at this guy. So young and vibrant and not dead inside. They discuss having the neighbors over for dinner and then decide against it with a conspiratorial laugh. A laugh, for Christ's sake. My father kisses my mother and walks out of the room. For my five-year-old self, this is normal. For my thirty-eight-year-old self, it is astounding. My mother and father together and happy. This is what I have been missing for so long. And it's been sitting in my head. How did I not do this sooner? Whatever it costs me, it's worth it. It is wonderful. And then it's gone.

I'm out.

My mother and myself and our kitchen and my father's footsteps and the tang of Sunday gravy in the air zip by me and I turn my head to follow but it's moving too fast. The memory is nothing significant and at the same time, it's everything. My mind is slaked. I had no idea it was this thirsty for knowledge. The void that is my childhood memory has one measly drop refilled. God, this feels amazing. It's over in an instant, but rich with more information than I can process. My home. My mother. My father. The smells. And then it was gone in the distance, a sliver of a universe that passed through me and left me alone in The White. My mother was beautiful and my father was in love and I was happy.

What was that?

I want more.

Another wail grows behind me only this one is bigger. Plural.

I turn my attention back around in time to see a tidal wave of memories screaming toward me. There are so many. The whoosh is more powerful this time. A tsunami of memories as tall and wide as I can imagine crashes over me. An explosion of imagery and sound blasts past me. Everything I have ever experienced flying by in bite size chunks, as if my brain is purging itself of the toxins that have poisoned it for so long. Vomiting up a lifetime of memories in an unfathomable volume of moving postcards arranged in no logical order. My first day of school. Driving in traffic. Sneaking out of Foster Parent's house. Buying groceries. Pouring coffee. Christmas morning. Oversleeping. Lisa's cunt best friend cornering me at a party to harangue me. Dropping my joint at a concert. Arguing with customer service. Buying a guitar. Riding the subway. Stealing a book. Opening a letter. Sneaking fruit through customs. Parallel parking. Millions of others.

Millions.

I want them all. I want to drink them all in. I know each one will taste just as good as the first and I will never be full. If I could grab them I would. But I have no body. I can't scoop them up and save them all to enjoy one at a time, savoring each long buried moment of my stupid, futile life.

The stoop.

Of the countless memories shooting by, one stands out by virtue of the pain associated with it. The memory of the stoop on the townhouse I lived in when I was eight years old. Four steps on the front of our building. The stoop where I would wait for my father to come home from work. The stoop where I played long-lost imaginary games with the neighbor kids while my bored mother watched and smoked. That awful, crumbling stoop that I stared at to avoid the eyes of my neighbors when the cops dragged my father out of our building.

And there it was. Passing by unaware of its significance to me. I must have it. Maybe I can't have all of them, but I want this one.

I focus my mind or whatever I have become on that one memory and manage to slow the streak of images down enough to watch this selected scene like a forgotten home movie unearthed at a relative's garage sale. I will it closer and demand it to keep playing. It moves toward me and through me and around me and then I'm in it.

Brooklyn.

Nineteen eighty-four-ish.

I was eight.

I am eight.

I'm there and I'm eight. Cop cars line the street in front of my building. Red and blue lights flashing. Some cops taking statements from the people who live next door. The neighbor who was always bitching at her husband talks to a uniformed policeman. She was a nosy one and has plenty to say. I'm sure it's all wrong and she's making most of it up but who would believe me if I opened my mouth? I can't hear her anyway. The rest of the neighbors mill around trying to figure out what's going on. They're right next to me but they feel like they're a million miles away.

I am the only person on earth who feels the way I do. I am an exhibit. This is a zoo and I am the only animal.

A fat cop wraps a blanket around me and tells me they're going to take care of me. I understand that I look like I just saw a ghost. I don't know where my sister is. A female cop is there. She seems disgusted with me. Or maybe she's worried. I want to ask her where my sister is and what will happen to us and what are they going to do with my father and when will this end but I don't because I don't think she'll answer. I'm convinced I'll get into trouble or, worse, she'll look at me with forced empathy and give me some bullshit, hope-filled answer that both of us know is a lie and then I'll be confused on top of scared.

So instead I'm silent as the zoo visitors stare at me. None of them take pictures but that's only because there's no way they'll ever forget this scene. The fat cop talks to the female cop like I'm not there. Like you talk to your daughter while you discuss feeding the monkeys even though the sign says in no uncertain terms not to.

—He's been through some shit. CPS is on the way.

—You know his father's on the job. Out of the sixth.

—No shit?

The fat cop looks back at a commotion coming from the house and I know I should keep looking at the bottom stair of the stoop. Instead I raise my eyes to see the front door of my building open and two New York City Coroner's office employees wheel out a gurney with a full body bag on it. My stomach sucks itself back to my spine but I can't look away. I watch the gurney all the way to the coroner's truck as they slam it into the bumper, collapse the legs, and shove it into the truck's gaping hole like a sofa being moved to a new apartment. This might be the ugliest thing I've ever seen and I can't figure out why I'm not angry. Neighbors react, some in shock, some with self-righteous acknowledgment, whispering their I-told-you-so's to each other and pointing across the street. I follow their know-it-all fingers to the cruiser I've been trying to not look at. Inside, my father sits, handcuffed from behind, tears streaming down his face. His eyes never leave mine.

I force myself to stare at my father while the gurney is strapped into the coroner's truck. When I hear them slam the doors shut, I mouth the words 'Thank you' to him as he sits there about to be taken away forever.

Thank you.

Finally, he cracks, rolling back against the seat, head flopping back and even through the closed window I can hear him sob.

And then I look away and find the bottom stair of the awful stoop. The neighbors still watch. They want me to cry. I won't. Not a tear.

The sound fades first. Then the colors begin to de-saturate. Soon, there is nothing left.

Black.

The memory is gone.

The White is gone.

My perfect, dimension-less body has regained weight and density and fatigue and pain and sorrow and regret. The memory storm is over. I am alone in the black with the chilling realization that I might still be alive.

(Oh my.)

The old boy gave it his best effort but succeeded only in the pusillanimous achievement of 'attempted' suicide. Again.

Another failure.

What would Arnold Rosen think? Or Dr. HackShag, for that matter? Or even Dr. Hirsch? Very little, I would guess. Something along the lines of it being a predictable course of action for a person in his condition. Followed by an *Oh well* or a *Such things happen* or perhaps even an . . . *Interesting* coupled with a stroke of the chin.

In any event, our man is alive with a cautiously optimistic prognosis of full recovery, which, if he proceeds along a traditional trajectory, will undoubtedly include questions, introspection, honesty, and realizations. Everything the old boy was hoping to avoid.

As the nurses cluck and the doctors grimace, our man lies in his hospital bed selfishly sucking up the time and energy of a dedicated staff while others embroiled in emergencies not of their own device suffer and call to the heavens to negotiate imaginary deals for their recovery or that of loved ones. The kinds of deals that are generally never heard and rarely honored. The kinds of deals that may not have been necessary were the proper resources available to them rather than having been exploited by our man who was too craven to entertain the idea of discharging a firearm into his mouth.

What a disappointing awakening our man has ahead of him. Oh yes, he'll wake up.

Remember, he failed.

17

I'm not in Heaven because there's a tube in my dick.

It's not Hell because the tube would be much larger.

Fuck.

I'm alive.

My eyes creak open. The hospital room is clean and cool and I can't move a muscle. Exhausted. Tubes in every orifice, not just my Johnson. Machines making beeps that mean something to someone. A pudgy nurse in the process of changing my IV bag. She smiles a beautiful smile that doesn't belong in a hospital. She must be new. I can see where the wrinkles and bags will be in five years if she lasts that long.

—Well, hello. We thought we lost you.

Her words are sweet, but I can tell she's speeding up the IV swap out so she can run and tell the doctor I'm not brain dead. I wonder who lost money on that one.

My eyes dart around the room. I'm assuming she's taking this as a good sign.

—How are you feeling?

How am I feeling? My eyes slow to a stop and I drift off into a thousand yard stare. The last thing I need is self-awareness, but now that she's asked the question I can't help but assess my current state. I am feeling terrible.

I'm too tired even to groan. My throat too dry to make any noise if I wanted to. I breathe a little deeper and hope she can translate that to mean that I'm feeling alive, for better or worse.

They thought they lost me. I was dead. I killed myself. Fucking finally.

And look what I found. I can see the room around me and I can see this highly trained, doughy woman looking at me like she cares what happens and I can see machines keeping me alive and the mound that is my feet at the end of the bed and the door to my room that's slightly ajar. But really, wherever I look all I see is the recollection of my lifeflash, the vast mental landscape of unexplored content that I am now aware of, its infinite potential soaking in to my consciousness. Tainting my perception of everything else.

My life.

I can see the real world around me, but I am now completely aware of the existence of the reality I thought I had destroyed. It's in there. All of it.

One recovered memory plays over and over in a constant loop, as if searching for approval or context or company. I was eight. Staring at the stoop. The night my father killed my mother. My god.

This is officially my earliest memory. HackShag has lost the title to the brash, young newcomer. Eight-year-old Christian Franco now holds the belt.

Chubs finishes up with the IV.

—Okay, you rest now.

Like I was going to enter the Ironman.

She scurries out to let the doctors know the good news.

I'm so tired.

Black.

18

*It's three years ago.

I'm standing in one of the ballrooms at the Four Seasons in Philadelphia.

I'm crying as two hundred Jews stare at me and think either *Oh, what a sweet young man* or *God, what a pussy*. Half of them are right.

I'm crying because I don't know what's going to happen next.

From what I can tell, men look at getting married as the end of a long, arduous process. Celebrating the end of the march of courtship. A culmination. Women look at it as a beginning. The launch party for your new life together. The starting line.

I'm crying because I don't know what's going to happen next.

I'm crying because I'm trying to remember how I got here and I can't.

I'm crying because I drank too much scotch before the ceremony.

I have no family at the wedding aside from my sister. My choice.

We're having a Jewish ceremony. I have no particular religious leanings beyond yelling the name of somebody's lord and savior when I stub my toe. On the other hand, Lisa was raised in a Jewish household. Orthodox, no less. Observed every holiday. Fasted. No crazy black dresses and wigs, but she went to Hebrew school and was bat mitzvahed. She still observed well into our marriage. Made the full spread for Rosh Hashanah every year. Tried to atone every Yom Kippur. Everything. But ask her what happened when you died and she'd tell you there's nothing. The lights go out. Black.

It made no difference to her that this one belief sort of negated the whole concept of practicing religion, Jewish or otherwise. If life only leads to black emptiness, how did practicing a religion help anything? It always struck me as pointless, but it was important to her so I said nothing. And now I have to stand here while this overblown donkey of a cantor murders a song I wouldn't like even if he could sing. It's endless.

When I saw Ella before the ceremony, she put on a brave face and wished me the best even though I know she has her doubts. And by doubts, I mean she thinks Lisa would make a delightful ex-fiancée. Ella's husband shook my hand and handed me another drink right before I walked to the chuppah. His little way of calling me a sucker. I was fine until I saw Ella waddle down the aisle with her maternity bridesmaid dress. How cruel of us, looking back. She didn't want to be in the wedding in the first place, but Lisa insisted and I bullied. Ella walked down the aisle with as much dignity as she could muster and all I can see is her rotund belly and I'm thinking maybe that will be Lisa one day and won't that make us whole? I could have held it in if I had kept my eyes closed the entire ceremony. Ella was my trigger.

I made it a point to have dinner with Ella and Tim as a foursome a few times before the wedding. We had never made the effort before then (also my choice), but I wanted to show off my new toy. This magnificent beast that I had tamed. This mountain I had climbed. Look what I did. I saw this beautiful creature and I snookered her into loving me almost as much as I love her. I broke her. Ella meet Lisa, my new life.

Ella forced a smile and talked girl talk with Lisa even though I know Ella well enough to understand that she was actually feeling Lisa out. Looking for the weak point. The cracks. Not that she would have ever acted on this intelligence. She knows better than to give me advice.

And here we are today.

I'm crying because I drank too much scotch before the ceremony and now it's starting to hit me that the last five months of hell are over. The planning and arguing and screaming and worrying about the wedding are done and we can finally get on with the crying and arguing and screaming of being married. This is the point at which my perspective intersects with Lisa's. This one day.

It's not sadness I'm feeling. It's relief.

I think I'm happy.

19

I wake again.

I'm still alive.

Still in the hospital.

Could have been an hour. Could have been two days.

There are fewer tubes and IVs. I'm able to sit up. The fat nurse with the great smile has been replaced by Harry who is not smiling. He's waiting. I reacclimate myself to the idea of being alive for the foreseeable future. Hmm. This could be an awkward conversation.

I know Harry's been picking up the slack for me at work. Covering for me with the other partners. Handling my bleating clients. Lying to them. Ordering underlings to do what I should have been doing and steaming about it the whole time. That's what I would have done. I wonder how long it took him to figure out I wasn't coming in. I doubt I was in any condition to ask the hospital to call him even if I could have remembered the number. Maybe they found my card in my wallet. Where's my wallet?

Have I been in here an entire week? Maybe.

Filling in the blanks, I realize Harry must have been calling my apartment and my cell and finally, just in case, the same hospital I was brought to last time. At least, I think that's where I am. Maybe he started with the hospital. He's a smart guy.

Harry looks terrible. Was he here all night? Watching me? Waiting for me to wake up? Hoping he would get one more chance to tell me what an asshole I am? What a guy. Fucking love this guy.

I wonder if I can talk. There's a feeding tube (a 'nasogastric' if I recall correctly the one malpractice suit I sat in on for kicks) running through my left nostril, down my throat, and into my stomach to feed me. My throat feels cramped and I want to rip the tube out but I know if I do that I'll never talk again. It might be worth it. I have nothing left to say to anyone.

Must have been at least a week. Maybe more. If I could raise my arm I would feel the stubble on my face to get a better idea. I'm too tired. And I don't really care. This must be costing someone a fortune.

Harry takes a deep breath and I know what's coming. He isn't here to shoot the shit or hold my hand or counsel me to put my faith in a higher power. He's angry. But I have no one else. I'll take angry.

Fuck it. I'll start and see how he reacts.

—I saw my father. I saw his face and I remembered that night. I saw it.

My voice is a whisper from the grave.

Harry waits a moment to let my statement register before disregarding it as information that is not relevant to him, as I am no longer relevant to him.

—You're fired. I thought I should tell you myself.

I'm not surprised nor do I feel a tinge of concern. I want him to know there are more important things to be dealt with. At the end of your life, you're not going to look back and thank the lord that you crammed those extra cases into your workload, Harry. Probate. Estate taxes. Money. It's all nothing. I saw my father last night. I was in the same room with him. Alive together. Listen to me for a second. Let's talk as one human to another.

—Harry . . .

—Good luck, Christian.

Harry turns and walks out and I am alone as if no one had ever been there.

20

(What's this?)

Our man has arrived back at his apartment upright and sober.

Having administered his own slightly premature dismissal from the hospital, he has bypassed countless liquor vendors along the way home, no doubt disappointing the local population of mixologists hoping for a despondent derelict to wile away an afternoon at the mercy of their skilled hands.

And to top that, our man initiated a grand total of zero unnecessary confrontations, arguments, or altercations in the six days he spent recovering in the private room his (now former) employer quietly paid for. None. Could he be saving up for something special? A prizefighter-esque banking of testosterone and rage for an upcoming title event?

What could be whirling about among the creaky gears of the old boy's cognitive machinations? A plan grander than his previous suicide by disgrace scheme? A notion that he may be, as they say in the B movie business, 'on to something'? Is that certain something in his eyes hope or defeat? Ambition or remorse? Acceptance or determination?

Let's look a bit closer.

Our man enters holding a bag from an art supply store and heads for the table in the middle of what you would refer to as his dining area, although he might think of it as the place where he finally resigned himself to the idea that his marriage was over before signing his divorce papers.

The loft, when he and his (then) wife bought it three years ago, was regarded as the height of design consciousness and the ideal backdrop for the handsome cosmopolitan couple. Minimalist with an assertive exactitude. Wide open with rooms delineated by furniture arrangements that self-dictated their own imaginary boundaries.

The kitchen ended approximately four feet beyond the bar stools that lined the far side of the marble topped island which had separated our man and his wife when she informed him she 'can't fucking take it anymore.'

The living room had as its centerpiece the sofa on which they sat silently for an hour as Lisa cried into her husband's loving embrace upon hearing the worst news of her life.

There was a magnificent view of SoHo at which our man gazed while contemplating the painful confrontation, bold honesty, and white-hot humiliation he would need to endure to repair the damage to his marriage (during the brief period when that option existed.)

The bedroom the once-happy couple shared was simply a king-sized bed at the west end of the loft surrounded by two night tables and artwork one would not be surprised to find in a master bedroom. Our man has slept on the couch since her departure.

But let us return to the business at hand, which appears to be illustration. Pads. Pencils. A hunch in the old boy's back that connotes either enthusiasm or anger. Our man is rather busy sketching and erasing and crumpling and sighing. Relentless, even.

But, why?

Therapy? Too bold of a play for our self-absorbed friend. Fun? It's hard to believe the old boy enjoys anything anymore. Artistic vision? Doubtful. Our man lacks the drive to tell stories to anyone other than the woman he is at any given moment attempting to bed and/or humiliate.

No, judging by the volume of discarded attempts he has already generated, this would seem to be an adventure in precision. A quest to generate a perfect vision known only to him for the purposes of preservation. A prophylactic endeavor to prevent his single newly recovered memory from dissolving into so many useless molecules.

What we are seeing is desperation.

21

I'm broke.

My credit cards are useless. My savings long ago carved up by New York's finest divorce lawyers. My checking account should have recently accepted a direct deposit of the last paycheck I will ever receive. And that is all there is and all that will be.

From what I understand, it takes about six months to evict someone from a rented apartment. I am unclear on the timeline of bank foreclosures if you own.

I don't even think about trying to find another job. I won't. Bruised, bitter, drunk, unmotivated. It goes without saying that I am unhirable. I'm broken. But, my plans are not the type that need long-term funding. If I'm careful, this final paycheck will cover me for the rest of my life.

I start with the eyes. That's the toughest part. You get that right and the rest is relatively easy. But you have to get the eyes right. The first sketches I draw are okay. But the eyes aren't right. So I start over again and again. I sketch ten and then twenty and then maybe a hundred pairs of eyes. My extra-wide bamboo flooring is covered in failed attempts.

I gave Lisa everything. Not at first. In the beginning, I fought like a cornered honey badger. I thought that's what love was. A slash and burn strategy. Look how bad I'm bleeding for you. Self-flagellation by attorney bills. Hers. Mine. Ours. Gone. Gone. Gone. The stocks were sold. The investments liquidated. A lot of cash burned through. I don't remember how much we had managed to save. Somewhere in the mid six figures, but that's all been reduced to ash. There came a point where

I understood that my plan would result in nothing beyond an upgrade of a perfect stranger's car and a transfer of my wealth to someone who honestly didn't deserve it. What wouldn't happen was a reconciliation.

One day I asked them to send papers with whatever they wanted on them and I signed the documents and sent them back without question. She kept everything but the highly mortgaged loft. I wonder if I can sell my overpriced flooring or trade it for food.

Finally, I begin to see something. The eyes that had begged my forgiveness so long ago stare back at me from the page. Soulful without apology, tragic without regret. My father's eyes.

Two hours later, using those eyes as a foundation, I have crafted an exact replica of one frame of the memory salvaged from my near-death lifeflash. Four hours after that, I am surrounded by complimentary sketches detailing the different components of the memory.

The stoop.

The neighbors pointing their nosy fucking fingers.

The cop wrapping a blanket around me while not shielding my eyes or distracting me or getting me out of the situation.

The blood splatter on my father's shirt.

The gurney clunking down the stairs without so much as a 'Pardon me.'

My father's shoulders awkwardly accommodating the handcuffs.

All of these things I had no memory of until yesterday. Together, they are a horrific collage, but I am satisfied.

It's after midnight.

I lay my worn pencil down on the table and stretch my back. I haven't eaten in at least twenty-four hours but take the matter no further than acknowledgment. The exercise is almost complete. I find the original drawing of my father's face and caption it with the words 'Thank You.'

Three minutes later, I'm face down on my thousand-count sheets for the first time in a very long time. They no longer smell like Lisa. I wish they did. I sleep for eighteen hours.

22

April 8, 1989

Dear Christian,

I hope this finds you well. I don't know if you're getting my letters or if you're reading them or if you hate me. I hope you're reading them. I understand if visiting is too difficult, but a note in return would mean the world to me. Please consider writing. Tell me about your life. Tell me every detail. Tell me what happens every minute of your day. Or tell me one thing. Send me a blank piece of paper.

As usual, I have nothing good to say about my experience here, and the details of my daily life are nothing a thirteen-year-old should ever hear so I will forgo any descriptions and continue my practice of sharing whatever memories I have in the hopes that you will know me as a father and as a man and as a human. I won't be alive forever and when I'm gone I hope that I can live on with you if only as the memories I have passed on through these letters.

I like to think there is a shoe box full of envelopes I have addressed to you under your bed or in your closet. It must be getting full by now. I imagine they are worn and dog eared and are a secret cache known only to you. I write to your sister as well, but she was so young when I went away I might as well be a stranger. I know she doesn't remember me and writes only as an obligation she feels for reasons I don't understand but am grateful exist. She's a wonderful child from what I can tell through letters and pictures. I hope that you are still taking care of her like you always did. I'll continue to believe you are until I hear different.

There were almost three of you. I'm sure you didn't know that. I planned to tell you later in life. But who knows what will happen and I don't like the idea of going to the grave with stories that no one else on earth knows. Stories that someone else should know.

When you were five and Ella was one, your mother became pregnant again. We didn't mean to have another baby just then. While your mother and I had always hoped to have a large family, money was tight at the time and another child in the home would have been very hard on us. The decision was a tough one, but I stood by your mother, and to be honest with you, I agreed with it. There are no records and no one knew but your mother, myself, and the gynecologist who performed the D&C so the reporters never found out about it, thankfully.

A year later, I had been promoted and we had made ourselves financially stable. But your mother was devastated by the abortion. I don't think she ever recovered. We tried for another child after a while but could never become pregnant again. I always wondered how much of that was physical and how much was psychological.

Your mother spiraled downward and away from us all slowly for years and by the time you were eight, I could no longer reach her. From there things escalated quickly and here we are.

I tell you this because I want you to know that she wasn't a bad person. She was a person who had bad things happen to her. As much as I tried to protect her, there are things that each of us must go through alone. I made my peace with our decision, but she could never get to the same place.

I sometimes wonder how life would have turned out different had we chosen to have that baby. People have done harder things. My partner came from a family of ten. Irish, of course. They made it work. What would that have meant for you to have a brother or another sister? What would it have meant for Ella? What if having the baby made your mother happy and none of this ever happened? What if the opposite happened and things got worse sooner? What if, what if, what if? Looking back I think we could have done it. I just don't know if that would have been a good or a bad thing. When you're young and everyone depends on you, you worry about everything. Later you look back and realize how ridiculous it all is. So much stress for nothing. Perspective is so often wasted on those of us who can do nothing with it. My point is that we made a decision based on what we thought was best for us as a family at the time.

This story might come as a shock or seem inappropriate, but as I have said, I don't know what lies ahead and I want you to know these things that I know. More importantly, I hope these letters paint your mother in a more positive light in your mind. She deserves it.

I love you every day.

Dad

23

(Oh, the audacity.)

On a certain level, one can't help but be impressed with the unabashed gall and gumption and ambition of our man as he enters the reception area of the good doctor he so recently abused. Consider the pluck of appearing without an appointment (or a shower, I might add) and expecting (demanding!) a receptive audience despite knowing very well that the schedule of a doctor of Arnold Rosen's caliber is invariably full to capacity.

Our man understands that a typical appointment is only fifty minutes, and therefore the remaining ten minutes of the hour, where we currently are, is patient free, theoretically leaving the doctor unencumbered. Our man has planned accordingly.

Not surprisingly, the doctor has his own agenda for this private time and uninvited interruptions are frowned upon, but this is of no concern to our man as he strides purposefully toward the inner office door.

The doctor's first line of defense does her part, attempting to slow the old boy's progress with the bold, efficient courtesy of a career receptionist who has dealt with the mentally volatile for years.

—Sir, can I help you?

Naturally, she is ignored and our man proceeds without hesitation leaving her in the modern predicament of wondering when physical force is acceptable.

24

I can't do this alone.

But the only qualified professional I know is that panooch psychiatrist I saw last week or whenever. He seemed like a smart guy for a pompous ass, so I figure he can help. He mentioned repressed memories right before I left. He must know something about it. More than I do.

I'm still recovering so I move like a caveman. Social conventions are meaningless. What do I care how people think of how I look? I have no manners. I am bereft of tact. I am an amorphous id in jeans and a tee shirt moving quickly through structures of glass and marble with a single focus. That's fine if you'd like to watch and point or perhaps take a video of me with your phone. Tell your kids about the weirdo you saw later when you sit at the dinner table. Laugh it up with the boys in accounting. I don't belong to that world anymore.

His secretary is on my heels, even though I'm already opening the door to his office.

—Excuse me, *sir*!

I walk in to find him sitting behind his know-it-all desk looking at his next patient's file. He's wearing a neck brace. What a pussy.

—Sir, you're going to have to make an appointment if you want—
The caveman ignores the worried little mosquito flitting behind him.

—We have to talk.

—I'm sorry, Doctor. I tried to stop him.

Arnold Fucking Rosen indicates it's okay. He appears to think he has the situation in hand, despite his neck brace. Like he was waiting for me even though I know he wasn't.

The secretary stands behind me for a second, I assume making wide-eyed faces at Arnold, encouraging him to get out of this situation. He's so busy taking me in and translating that to opportunity he won't look at her.

—We're fine, Elise. Thank you.

Finally, she backs out but I know she's already dialing nine, one, and preparing to hit that last one upon the slightest provocation.

He looks at me like I'm fascinating. I haven't even thought about checking a mirror lately. I must look like a maniac. Maybe that will work for me. Look at me, Doc! Can't you see the potential? Think big. Think book deal. Arnold versus the Caveman. It's got a nice ring to it.

—Hello, Christian.

—The other night. I almost died. And as I'm fading out, I saw something. Something important.

I hold up the sketch. The one with the eyes and the Thank you. It shakes in my hand when I hold it up, but only a little. In the time honored style of Arnold Rosen, I get no response.

—It's my father. I told you I couldn't remember anything before I was nine years old. But I did. This is it. My father's face. From when I was eight. And I know there's more in there.

I'm pointing at my head. In there. That's where there's more. In the caveman's melon.

Rosen glances at the drawing. He takes his sweet time before he answers.

—I'm sorry. I was told your employment at Hunter & Partners had been terminated.

—So?

—So they pay my fee. I had an arrangement with Harry.

—I'll pay.

—I'm five hundred dollars an hour. Up front. And this type of therapy could take years.

I'd pay five thousand an hour for this. I wonder how fast I can sell my apartment. Maybe I can sign it over to him. It's still worth something and I think I made my last mortgage payment. I'll sleep in the park.

—I could . . .

—Christian, my schedule is already full. And honestly, I was doing Harry a favor.

Dr. Rosen rubs his neck through the brace. His other hand is under his desk and I wonder if he has a gun. I wonder if he bought a gun because of the quality time we spent together. Is that what you did, Arnold Rosen?

He smiles a weak smile as he lies to me.

—Really, I'm sorry.

As a caveman, I know I have the option of crushing his skull with the oversized ceramic brain paperweight on his desk. That's what cavemen do when they're provoked. I have a priority, though, and crushing skulls isn't it. Neither is getting arrested. So, Arnold Rosen, please wallow in all the snarky, interpersonal one-upmanship you'd like. I fold. My focus is singular and if you're not going to help me, I'll move on. Like a caveman.

I pass a couple of cops on my way out. They give me a quick onceover but then hustle along to the office of a respected psychiatrist whose assistant called a few minutes ago.

25

*It's two years and nine months ago.

I'm blowing out Lisa's hair.

She could get it done by her guy, but she says I'm better. I'm not, but I like doing it.

She's fresh out of the shower, wrapped in her robe. No carefully applied makeup. No signature perfume. No tailored clothes. Just Lisa. She smells wonderful. Sitting in front of her mirror. Patiently waiting for me to do what I do. We've got plenty of time before we have to be anywhere.

Things have calmed to a dull predictable roar between the two of us, as I believe they do with most legally committed couples. We wake up together and leave for our jobs and come home around the same time (she works as hard as I do) and might even be enjoying the early grooves of what will hopefully soon be a deep rut.

I've got the top three-quarters of the left side of her mane twisted around and clipped up and I'm working on the bottom quarter. You have to get the bottom straight before you move to the top sections. It's the foundation. This part usually takes the longest but it's a good warm up for the finesse involved in the top layers. This is my system. You have to get the foundation straight or you're wasting your time. A wet foundation will get the hair you've dried on top of it damp enough that it will start to wave. So do the foundation first. The foundation is everything.

I'm transforming her.

Blowing her hair out takes about a half an hour, but while we're in the thick of it, time is nonexistent. It could be a minute. It could be a day. The sound of the dryer creates a protective cocoon of sound around us, tells the rest of the world to fuck right off. The heat bouncing back reminds me this is where I should be. Right here.

Occasionally, she'll look up from the gossip rag she's reading and smile. I smile back although I'm so focused I'm sure it looks like a smirk.

I tend to underestimate the range of my facial expressions. What feels like a broad smile to me looks like a wan grimace to its recipient. Pure shock comes off as mild amusement. Anger as grating irritation. I noticed the tendency when I looked at pictures in which I thought I was perhaps smiling too much. I wasn't. The interpolation to other expressions wasn't too tough. I checked in my bathroom mirror to confirm the hypothesis—yes, when I made a super happy face I looked sardonic, when I acted depressed I looked bored. That explained a lot. I was twenty-seven when I figured this out and there was already a mass grave of emotional disasters I could easily attribute to my underperforming face. I decided to do nothing about the issue. What could I do, after all? Overact? Fake emotion? To what end? You get what you get and that's it.

Lisa's expressions are the opposite. Easy. Quick. Transparent. Exactly what she's feeling. When she's happy, she looks happy. When she's sad, she looks sad. I won't go so far as to say she has a simple interior life because she's too smart for that. She's complicated and thoughtful, but has an amazing capacity to leave things in the past. While I will let a grudge echo into other emotions long after its causal event has been forgotten, she releases grievances without a second thought, moving on with zero baggage. It's admirable.

There was a time when Lisa thought my smirk was adorable.

I finish with the foundation of her hair and release one of the top quarters from its clip. You have to work fast here, as you don't want the damp hair corrupting your foundation. You want to build on top of what you have so as to create a seamless configuration. And that means pulling smaller sections tight with your rounded brush, quickly heating them straight and moving on. Confident baby steps.

Earlier she asked how my day was and I told her it was fine. I told her some of the boring details and she reciprocated with stories equally forgettable. I helped with some mundane negotiation. She started a new line. I had lunch with a potential client. She hired a new assistant. We're weaving our lives together with the fine threads of everyday existence.

This blow out should last until at least Friday. After that, it's done. Disposable. And I'll start all over again.

The sun fries my face like an egg.

It's four or five in the afternoon. I've been passed out for at least twelve hours. My boxers are soaked with urine. My eyes are still puffy from the crying. I sort of remember sobbing loudly. The empty gallon bottle of vodka lies on its side next to my head. Not sure how much I drank and how much spilled out. Probably a lot of both. The self-hypnosis book I stole from the discount bookstore sits on the floor in front of me. Ineffective even with the booze greasing the wheels.

I strip naked and stick my open mouth under the faucet in the kitchen for a good two minutes. So dehydrated when I woke up. And now I'm bloated. Gluttonous no matter what I'm doing. It physically hurts to hear things like traffic and wind and my own footsteps. I can feel my eardrums. I remind myself to boost some Pedialyte today.

The hypnosis book is open to chapter five. I remember reading the first two chapters and thinking I understood the basic concepts, but like so many past pursuits, I'm sure I gained just enough knowledge to be dangerous and jumped in head first. I bet I skimmed three and four and read the title of five before I tried the technique on myself.

My pores are leaking vodka. I'm sweating 100-proof potato water.

The plan was to force myself to become relaxed enough to tap into those long-lost memories that I now know are there. Billions of them. I wish I had a power drill to put a nice tight hole in my head to relieve the pressure in there by letting all the missing sights and sounds of my childhood out one by one. I'd put the hole right between my eyes so I could watch them fly free.

My logic was that if I got drunk fast enough I'd find that sweet spot of inhibition in which this hypnosis nonsense would work. I could trick myself. I know before I pick up the drawings I made last night that I failed.

They're garbage. Artistic ramblings hoping to spark memory. No new memories. No new insights. No epiphanies.

I remember sitting at the table, reading. Focused. Waking up forgotten mental muscles. At one time in my life I was a good student. A great student, in fact. For seven years I managed to channel my unrecognized anger into studying. Graduated college like a rap star finishing a concert. I knew I had killed it and if there was a mic to go along with my diploma I would have slammed it to the ground. Law school was harder but I only took that as a challenge. I was impudent with my intelligence. Willful in my determination.

Fuck you if you think you can stump me.

Hell yes I want the extra-credit assignment.

Move out of my way and let me answer in your place, you simp.

I remember fondly when my rage was a highly refined tool. There was even a trickle-down effect to my work style.

Damn right, I'll work late.

Sure I thought of that thing you'd need but didn't realize you would need it so soon.

Yes, I saw the hesitation in your eyes and moved in before you could.

At one point, I had a very dangerous mind.

Last night I succeeded in doing nothing but getting drunk.

I pick up my earlier drawing of my father and stare at his eyes like he's going to tell me something. Get yourself together. Keep going. Stop. Fuck you.

Like I said, I can't do it alone.

27

If you were only three when all that shit went down, you probably turned out okay.

Who remembers anything from when they were three? Your first thirty-six to forty-eight months on Earth all fade into gauzy clouds of cerebral detritus before you're ten, more feelings than recollections. Familiar neural connections rather than logical storylines and clear pictures. Fluff.

When you're that young, your brain is terribly impressionable. Neuroscientists use the term 'plastic.' At that time your cerebral cortex had well over a hundred trillion synapses. Gray matter galore. Far more than you knew what to do with. You probably stored the memories of that one night in pristine HD and surround sound. For a while, anyway. Oh, the machinations of your little three-year-old brain, whirling away as it tried to figure out the whys and wherefores of exactly what happened. Holy cats. The hours you must have wasted replaying the scene.

But here's the thing. You spent the following years reducing your overall number of synaptic connections to a more manageable amount. That's a process called pruning. You cut out the stuff you don't need to make room for the stuff you do. Your body went to work like a sculptor, taking a good look at the raw material in its workspace and cutting out anything unnecessary. This went on until you were around eight. At that point you had the brain structure you were going to have into adulthood. Yes, you continued to fill it with whatever information was around or was force-fed to you by the public school system and prime time television, but the mechanics of how your brain worked and what activities it was optimized for were firmly established.

If you were only three, there's a chance that your brain was smart enough to prune out the memories of your mother's screams and your father's rage or the time you were left alone for thirty-two hours. Wiped them out in favor of something like mathematical aptitude or spatial relations or a sense of humor. Things you might actually need.

If you were only three, then you wouldn't have gone to the same therapist as your older brother who was already eight and who's brain was done pruning and was so very active and so very fertile and could understand the physics of how guns worked and how people didn't once they were shot in the head. No, you would have had a very different experience that didn't include a low-rent public servant who decided to go into social work when his substitute teacher gig didn't work out. You would have been watched, of course. Monitored. Conversations would have been had with your foster parents (at least with the half who did the actual fostering) to see if there were any red flags The City should be aware of. But eventually, the questions and the monitoring would stop because if anything drastic were going to manifest, it would have done so already. Or so the thinking went back then.

Certainly you must have enjoyed the sensations of undying love for your parents no matter how unpredictable or unreliable the two of them were. That's what three-year-olds do. But that phase of your life ended early enough that it was still possible to reduce those feelings to a vague little sigh of memory or perhaps even wipe them out completely. Not suppress them, mind you. Suppression would have involved a lot more work and years and years of effort and behind-the-scenes psychological strain to make sure nothing ever leaked out. Suppression would have meant other things had to be sacrificed—like empathy or vulnerability or self-esteem or the ability to commit—to make room for all those horrible memories you would be keeping locked so deep in your head. Thankfully, the mental tool of suppression wasn't in your brain's skill set yet.

If you were only three when your mother died a horrible senseless death while you cried and no one stopped it, there's still a good chance that you grew up to be a relatively healthy thirty-three-year-old living out on the island with an understanding husband who works as a sports agent and is a pretty good father to your young children, one of whom happens to be around three herself right now. Chances are your children have given you a lot to think about as they passed this benchmark (for you) age and you have wondered how they would have reacted to the loss of a parent at the hands of another parent. It must be heartbreaking to picture it happening to your children even though you never seem to think of yourself as damaged goods. But you're tougher than them, no? Tougher or angrier? You probably don't know how bad other people think your temper is. Or maybe you do but you figure this is simply the disposition you were born with and there is nothing to be done about it. Could be.

You're probably still in touch with your brother thirty years later although it's a good bet you choose to keep him at arm's length now that he's become so morose and self-destructive. That's called compassion fatigue. You get the same thing when you watch too much cable news coverage of whatever big world disaster happens to catch our collective attention. After a while you want whoever it is that's afflicted with this ungodly pain to shut the fuck up and move on. Sound familiar? Sorry about the whole Tsunami/Earthquake/Survivor Guilt thing, but I've got shit to do.

In all probability, you'd rather your brother was one of the guys and came out to watch the game with your husband and ate wings and drank beer and acted like the fun uncle you always hoped he'd be. Can't he keep his compulsive behavior and panic attacks to himself like everyone else? But dollars to donuts you also understand that's never going to happen, as his experience was quite different than yours and that made him a different person although how he let his marriage fall apart like that you'll never get.

Statistically speaking, you're likely to be relatively healthy mentally and what you know of that one dark night comes only from the police reports you tracked down once you accepted that your father was never going to talk about it no matter how many times you visited him and begged. Oh, and from the newspaper articles that are now conveniently online and so very available for your review after your husband goes to sleep. But that's really it. All you know is what some strangers wrote down. Because you don't remember anything. You were only three.

Lucky you.

28

(Well, well, well.)

The old boy is reaching out for some much needed hand holding from a loved one. Maturity or foolhardiness? Hard to say for certain, but let's adopt a positive outlook and call it progress. A nice first step, yes?

Do attempt to ignore the sullen face our man has adorned himself with as he stares out the window of the train. Surely, it's more unguarded passion than intentional pose. Most likely, he's steeling himself for his impending visit with his estranged sibling. Unpleasant doesn't begin to describe what he anticipates might happen.

One would hope that his attitude has nothing to do with his resentment of the perfection his sister appears to have attained in her personal life. Based on the landscaping of her front lawn alone, it would be easy to presume a world of personal contentment and happiness punctuated by warm hugs from her children and meaningful winks from her handsome husband. As an outsider you could easily be forgiven for thinking that, as a wife and a mother, she has transcended.

You wouldn't be wrong. Superficially, anyway. Ella's children kiss her hello and goodbye without prodding. Her husband brings home flowers at random intervals, making sure she knows that the motivation behind them is none other than his undying love for the woman he married so long ago. It is a world she has cultivated as carefully as her gardener weeds her rose garden.

But this is not to say there isn't a crackling underlying current of anxiety. Pay close attention to her hands when the phone rings. They tense quickly as if any call could be the one that turns her life upside down. Watch her eyes as she scans her own quiet suburban street while she washes the dinner dishes. She's not enjoying the view. She's keeping an eye out. Visit her bedroom before the dawn breaks and you'll find she has no need for an alarm clock. She is awake, thinking thoughts she will never share even with the man sleeping next to her. The condition has worsened over the recent months, although subtly enough that Ella herself is not aware of her own increased level of agita.

Even if she had the inclination, she could not tell you the cause for this never-ending torque of anxiety twisting her consciousness at all hours. She might refer to herself as high-strung, although her closest girlfriends would laugh and say *That's just Ella!* But there is genetically wired anxiety and there is man-made, unconscious, low-grade terror of forgotten childhood trauma. That is not just Ella.

29

*It's two years and four months ago.

I'm in Vegas for my friend Jack's bachelor party.

We're on the top of the Luxor or the Venetian or the Wynn in a penthouse that must have cost him a shitload, but none of us care. There are four or five whores running around the suite and on the table in front of me there's a mound of coke the size of a fat baby's head. I'm indulging in neither so far.

I'm appropriately drunk for the occasion and continuing the process without a governor. That's what you do. Someone calls for a round of shots. I think it was the blonde with the outline of Texas tattooed above her left hip. She's rented by the hour and, apparently, her game is to consume as much booze and coke as possible. Oh, and dicks. I've seen her go into the back bedroom with at least three of my friends so far tonight. Yes, one of them was Jack.

I'm handed a shot and down it without thinking, as I'm in a rabid discussion with a fellow attendee regarding the merits of a new Yankee relief pitcher. The blonde sits on my lap and tries to flirt with a thick southern accent that must work on some guys but only makes me think she's super-racist or an idiot or both.

—Who wants a blow job?

Her perfume is making my eyes water. In tasteful doses it's probably delightful, but she has absolutely marinated herself in the stuff and from this brief interaction alone I know I'll still smell like her three days from now.

Honestly, as hot as she is, I'd rather finish making my point than get head from this idiot so I slide her off my lap without too much interaction beyond politely declining.

—Thanks, maybe later.

The guy I'm talking to looks at me like I'm crazy and accepts the offer she didn't make him.

—Fuck, I do.

The whore cuts a thick line, snorts it up, and grabs the guy's hand, dragging him back to the bedroom. As they leave, she asks him if he has cash. He asks if she can break a hundred.

I don't have a specific moral code in terms of prostitutes. I'm fine with them and have paid for sex a few times when the occasion seemed right. Like a bachelor party. But I'm not feeling it tonight.

I head for the kitchen to grab another beer and notice I'm unsteady on my feet. I wonder how many shots I've had. No clue.

Five minutes later (I'm guessing), I'm talking to the goth whore and she's laughing hysterically.

Later we're playing beer pong and the goth chick is topless. Jack is passed out and someone got arrested I think.

The last thing I remember is throwing a lamp out the window to see if I could hit the pool. I did. The goth whore thought it was hilarious.

The rest is gone. Blackout.

I wake up at three o'clock the next afternoon.

The whores are gone. The coke is gone. There's no more booze. There's no money in my wallet. Lisa won't answer my calls or texts. I check my phone to see if I called her the night before. I'm assuming I said something dumb or picked a fight or something.

Ah.

Looks like there was an outgoing call to our home number placed right before ten thirty last night. And it went on for forty-eight minutes. No way I talked to her for that long in the middle of a bachelor party. Plus I was relatively sober at that point. I remember arguing about baseball around that time. It takes a second, but my rickety brain finally figures out that I pocket-dialed Lisa. My phone was in my front pocket having been used to dial up ERA stats to buttress my inane argument. She was my last call before the party. An accidental redial.

Smooth.

I reconstruct what I can of what she might have overheard, but I can't remember all of it so I have to go with what I know of myself and deduce my actions based on past performance.

I probably didn't do any coke. If I did, I'd still be up. She hates when I do coke. Doesn't like the person I become. I don't either but it feels so fucking good.

I probably didn't say anything bad about Lisa. I tend to keep that to myself and unsheathe it when we're alone together, so chances are I wasn't mouthing off about her last night.

I probably didn't fuck that goth whore. She was smoking hot and mine for the asking but I don't think I did it. My fingers don't smell like anything but cigarette smoke. No latex. No vagina. I probably didn't do anything.

So that puts my mind at ease somewhat. The bigger problem will be convincing Lisa that nothing happened. I doubt she'll be interested in smelling my fingers.

I could roust Jack and the other guys and ask them but that opens a Pandora's box I don't want to look into. They'll either lie about me fucking all the whores to break my balls or confirm that I nailed the goth girl for real. Not interested in going any deeper down that path. I'm fine with my own investigation and decide to leave it at that.

I lie back on the couch and try to sleep this off until the rest of the crew wakes up. We've got an eight o'clock flight tonight.

God dammit.

30

I'm standing outside Ella's house.

It's easily four thousand feet of smarmy family-oriented accoutrement. A good inch and a half of edging between the grass and the curb. Alarm company sign planted boldly before the front hedges. Volvo in the driveway next to a Lexus. Jesus. How safe can you play it?

She opens the door and it's obvious she saw me walking up the drive. I don't fit into her schedule. Probably messing up her Yogalates lesson or whatever. I should have shaved.

—Christian. What are you doing here?

My niece runs up and grabs her mom's leg. She's three.

—Who's that, Mommy?

—This is your Uncle Christian, Sarah. You were probably too young to remember meeting him.

Sarah is too shy or smart to say hello to me. She looks like her mom, only happy and unguarded.

—Hi, Sarah. You got big.

I'm worn out already from this minor, phony attempt at pleasantry. Ella dismisses Sarah and stands aside. I guess she's letting me in. She doesn't move too far from the door or let go of the handle, so I guess she's only letting me in briefly.

—So?

—I have to talk to you. About Dad.

Ella deflates. I might as well have punched her in the stomach. This is unfair. I should have called first. But, then she would have told me not to come or made sure to be gone when I did. Besides, she has no idea what's been going on and it's not like I can explain my situation over the phone.

—You look terrible.

—I've been remembering things.

Ella sighs and looks much older than when she opened the door. But she still plays dumb. She hates talking about this. When she was a teenager it was all she talked about. She was so angry. All the black clothes and dumb haircuts and bad boy crushes and cutting. I probably should have been more open to discussing it, but I couldn't back then. I can barely do it now. Later when the Internet made things too easy to resist temptation, I know she scoured newspaper sites for old articles and rumors. I know she found plenty because when she did get me to talk about things, she knew far more than she did when she was younger and none of it was anything I had told her. Because I never told her anything.

—What kind of things?

This will be exactly as hard as I expected it would be. The only question is do I have the balance of stamina and patience to wear her down. I know she won't respond to anger so I leave that at the front door and go with quiet honesty.

—Things from the night he shot her. I want to know—

Ella switches quickly into Desperate Housewives mode. She smiles and clasps her hands together. I'm being *handled*.

—Oh, Christian. We've been over this. I told you I remember nothing. I can't help you like you want me to. I'm happy to listen and I'll always be here for you, but I can't answer questions. I don't remember and it was a long time ago. Are you hungry?

She moves toward the kitchen. I follow, but slowly. This will end badly within the next two minutes. The splinters of my mind that still function race to think of something/anything to turn the tide as she prattles on, avoiding my purpose.

—You're in luck. I made brownies. Double fudge. Tim loves them. He'll be here any minute. Maybe you two can watch the game together. Do you still like good cigars?

I have nothing but the single track I came in on. I am too focused for much tact or strategy or couth. I know this is a waste of time but there is no one else. I have to say the words.

—I need you to think back.

Ella stops. She's holding back.

—Maybe you should leave.

—But you were there. I know you remember.

—No. I wasn't. There's nothing to tell you.

—Yes, you w—

Ella hurls a plate at my head. I don't move. It misses my face and hits the wall next to me. She screams and I know she's thinking of something that I'll never see.

—I DON'T REMEMBER!

She remembers. I fucking knew it. I just have to convince her to talk to me.

I'll be back.

31

*It's two years and two to four months ago.

    —I'm sick of this shit.

    —I already told you why.

    —We need to talk about this.

    —You're not listening to me.

    —Why is it always my fault?

    —You're not being fair.

    —That's not what I said.

    —I'm done with this conversation.

    —You're twisting my words.

    —Why do you insist on pulling this shit?

    —That's what you said last time.

    —You're not going anywhere.

    —Then maybe you should just do that.

Chemistry. That was always our problem. No matter how hard we fought it, we always had chemistry.

32

(Well, it's about time.)

The old boy positions himself delicately on the chair. You know how persnickety modern furniture can be. He's attached his noose to the same bar on which he used to perform chin-ups for the entertainment of his wife. It's already proven to handily bear his weight and so should serve as a smashing good gallows today.

His front door has been made to allow easy entry and a small ruse has been arranged to prevent the neighbors from interfering with the emergency response team's entrance.

Our man positions the rope carefully about his neck, rings up the authorities and makes known his situation.

—Hi, I'd like to report an attempted suicide. Would you please send an ambulance to one thirteen Prince street, apartment seven B, as in boy. . . . That's correct, 'boy.' Thank you. Oh, and please hurry. . . . No, I can't.

Like a well-oiled machine. Two minutes and twenty-five seconds to go.

33

I kick away the chair I'm standing on, fall, and hang by my neck.

It hurts more than I thought it would. Good.

I'm stone-cold sober so I'm scared out of my fucking mind. The noose ends up positioned nicely, which is lucky because if it lands wrong it will break your neck and then you've defeated the whole purpose of the effort. I try not to struggle, although it's tough to stop the most primitive part of my brain from making my body wriggle around. I'm gasping for air even though the last thing I want is to breathe right now. I can't help it. I try to focus on something else. Think about baseball. Think about car repair. Think about Lisa.

That's the real agenda here, isn't it? Lisa by way of rehabilitation? Restoration of my self?

No. Not restoration. I'm a tear-down. I need to be razed and rebuilt from scratch if I have any chance at all. Reconstructed, only this time with integrity and honesty and all the care and planning that wasn't there the first time around. And none of the scars.

I need tools. I need a blueprint. I need my insides stripped and laid bare to see what I have to work with. What was there before? Where are the cracks in the foundation? What's clogging up my emotional air ducts?

I've been given an opportunity. A chance.

This will work or it won't. My master plan. If it works, I have the key to everything. I can fix what I've broken so badly. I can alter my fundamental being and become the man Lisa thought I was. The man that, at least for a while, she believed I could be.

If I succeed, I can change.

If I fail, then it doesn't matter. Either way, the issue has become one of black and white. Black, I'm gone. White, I win.

If it doesn't go as I hope, what will be the last thing I ever see? The bed I used to share with Lisa? The night table she left her earrings on? The empty half of the closet I haven't used since she left? Is it possible to look at nothing? I wish I had nothing in this apartment. I wish it were bare and empty and alone. It should be. It deserves it.

I've been up here a full minute and I'm only now getting tunnel vision. I'm doing it wrong. There's too much oxygen getting to my brain. My neck must be in a position that allows some air to get through. Dammit.

I raise my arms to grab the rope above the noose and hoist myself up a little to readjust. The tension in my throat goes away and I can't help but suck in a huge breath. Oh, that feels so good. Best breath I ever took. My biceps are already aching from holding myself up. Maybe I should pull my head out of this and rethink the plan. No. I was afraid leaving my arms unbound might lead to this. Doubt. Weakness. Not now. Don't be scared. Don't give up. You have a plan. Stick with it. Let go.

I turn my head slightly, lower myself slowly into a position that I know instantly will kill me. Not a molecule of oxygen is getting through and I'm too weak to lift myself again. This is it. I think my body is wrenching around involuntarily but I can't be sure because I'm not even positive I'm here anymore. My brain screams adrenaline at me but my mind whispers sweet nothings right back. Relax. This is what you want.

The room sways back and forth a few times before the view begins to defocus again. Quicker this time.

Sound fades away.

My vision dims.

Yes.

Black.

34

Silence.

The White.

I'm back.

Whatever I am is naked and fresh. It feels so good. Better than I remember.

I love it here. I love it so much.

I couldn't feel anger if I tried. I have no ego to crush. I love you.

I hear the whisper and then the wail and then the whoosh.

Ten thousand express trains of memories race past me. I have no body. I am pure concentration. I am a flat line. I am complete.

I look to my right and strain to slow the images. I'm successful enough to see my ninth-grade baseball tryouts.

Waiting in line for my coffee.

Watching the cable guy work in my apartment.

Sitting on hold.

Biking by the river.

Waking up in a stranger's bed.

Cheating in high school chemistry.

Showering.

Playing basketball.

Buying a paper.

Lying in a crib.

I turn to my left to see myself changing a channel.

Skipping class.

Running late for work.

Laughing at Stern.

Yawning.

Fighting with an ex-girlfriend.

Sitting on a subway.

I lean back. There are just as many images flying above me. I'd stay here forever if I could. In a second it will all be over.

There. My childhood house. The laundry room.

I focus.

It's March of whatever year I was eight.

I'm terrified.

Hiding in the corner behind a laundry basket. I'm watching my mother as she cries, staring at the locked door as she crouches next to the washing machine, terrified. The room is hot from the dryer. The washing machine is spinning an unbalanced load, making too much noise and offering too little protection. Her dress is a light floral pattern that seems familiar to me. She's swimming in it. Must be fifteen pounds lighter than the last memory I saw her in. Oilier hair. Deeper lines in her face.

BOOM! BOOM! BOOM! Someone is pounding on the door. It might break.

It's my father. He's yelling through the hollow wood.

—Let me in there, God dammit! Open this fucking door or I'll break it down!

BOOMBOOMBOOM! The door cracks a little at the top. The hinges are loosening from the door frame. My mother can't stop shivering. She's wearing house slippers and they're filthy as if she might have been wearing them outside as well. The smell of her perfume mixed with her sweat wafts my way. I have to remember this part. How the fuck do I sketch a scent?

She looks back my direction but I don't think she sees me. Her eyes are wide like an animal's.

—Open up!

She grabs the sides of her head and screams. My eight-year-old self wipes a full palm of sweat beads from my forehead. How long have we been in here?

—Leave me alone! Why can't you leave me alone!

She curls up tighter on the floor and convulses with sobs. I'm watching. Helpless. Paralyzed.

She looks up at me. She does see me. Talks to me like I'm an adult.

—Why won't he leave me alone?

I have no answer for her. She sobs and my father beats on the door.

I can't hold on much longer. I look around and force myself to remember every detail. The cluttered shelves. The sound of her sniffles. The vibration of the off-kilter washing machine. The heat of the dryer. The feel of the tension coming from the door. Everything.

And then it's gone.

Black.

35

An ambulance siren.
    I'm strapped down.
    I'm bursting through hospital doors.
    My clothes are ripping.
    Someone yells *Clear!*
    A PHOOMP of defibrillator paddles.
    A heart monitor beeps once and my soul smiles.

I did it.

Black.

    I wake up. Tired in my bones.
    I move my eyes enough to look around the room. This must be a community or teaching or whatever kind of hospital is the dirtiest. Very different from my last stay. Isn't there a code hospitals have to adhere to? I feel like SoHo should have something nicer to service its ill and deranged. At least something hip. But this place is a dump. Someone should be fired.
    There's an old guy in the bed next to me. Coma. Gotta be.
    An orderly changes coma guy's sheets like he's fixing a flat. Not what you would call rough, although not overly concerned with his patient's comfort. But what's the old guy going to say? He's probably never going to wake up. I wonder if he's wallowing in his own memories? Living in

The White. Did he figure it out? Is he leisurely traipsing through his own childhood? Or is he sleeping off a tough life in The Black? Either way, I'm a bit envious.

The real question is how many times can I pull this off? It's draining like nothing I've ever felt, but I already know I'll do it again. I can still smell the fabric softener. I can see every wrinkle in my mother's face. I can feel the grit on the floor. How long until it fades? The edges are already crumbling. How much of the story have I lost?

Two doctors look over my file. Their backs are to me. I don't say anything.

—He's lucky he didn't break his neck.

—I.D.?

—John Doe. No wallet. I think someone's checking with the building manager to get a positive I.D. At least we know where to send the bill.

What are the chances they'll let me borrow a pencil and a sketch pad? I'd settle for a hypodermic and a clean sheet and draw in my own blood if I could start right now. Every second counts. Man, are they taking their time.

—Bellevue?

—Any family to admit him?

—Nah. He's a loner. This'll have to be involuntary.

—You gonna sign for it?

—Go ahead.

—I'll shoot you for it.

Then they actually shoot for it, the fucks. The Indian doctor loses and I can tell he's pissed about it. I don't want him changing my sheets.

They look back at me but my eyes are closed. Saw that coming.

—Fucking broken people. I'll make the call.

—Let's get him out today. We need the bed.

They leave to go make some other important medical decisions and perhaps roshambo in the event of a disagreement on a diagnosis.

So this is it. Fuck Bellevue.

I force myself to sit up. Don't see my clothes anywhere. I pull the needles and tubes out of my arms and hop out of bed as fast as a guy who was dead for forty minutes can move. Which is not very fast.

Coma guy has some clothes hanging in his cubby. Cheap fucking place can't even put doors on the closets. He's a little shorter than me, and his shirt smells like old man sweat but they're close enough. There are no shoes. I don't care. I just need to get home without being arrested.

I have work to do.

36

(Hmm.)

Say what you will about the careless manner in which the old boy conducts his life, but there can be little doubt that our man is nothing less than dedicated to his newfound artistic vision. A conservative estimate would put the number of drawings he has output since his last death at sixty-five. Granted, not all of them are Louvre-worthy. I remind you these are the product of a man whose most recent previous work consisted of a compilation of marginalia featuring respected business colleagues fellating one another amidst innumerable scatological references dashed off in the sidelines of what should have been professional, detailed notes. Hardly a collection to set off a bidding war among the Rothschilds.

But this.

This assemblage of captured memories our man has generated is nothing short of impressive. The perspective is memorable. The style is distinct. The passion is undeniable. This is the work of a man driven by a vision that is positively insistent.

Or it is vain lunacy. Who's to say?

37

I keep going.

More drawings.

The door.

The laundry room.

The yelling.

I'm sitting at my kitchen counter aware that my lower back is aching but unwilling to stretch until I get these last details right.

The pounding.

The hinges.

The pleading.

The tears.

The anger in my father's voice.

The heat.

How do I draw heat?

I don't draw myself because I don't know what I looked like. I am the missing puzzle piece, but I'm also the least important one. I have no idea what I was at this time in my life. Or anytime before it. There are no pictures of me that young. Or there were but they're gone now. Probably at some point someone loved me enough to take my picture, but, to my knowledge, no proof exists to support this theory. My father's personal effects from jail were minimal and did not include photos of either of his children. Seemingly, a result of his overwhelming guilt.

If pictures of us were kept around the house, I wouldn't know. I never went back after my mother died. Never took anything personal from the place. Not a picture. Not a toy. Not a teddy bear. Someone must have taken my clothes for me or maybe they bought me new ones.

I assume my family's apartment was left to rot with no one to pay the mortgage. How long did the place sit empty before it was cleared out, pictures and all, and auctioned off to a stranger? Who would buy it after all that? Somebody. It's New York.

My mother's eyes. Her posture. The cower. The fear. The desolation. She was scared for her life.

There must have been at least one picture of me, but I'll never see it. What I looked like doesn't make a bit of difference. A fraidy cat little shit probably. That's not important for what I'm doing here. What I need is every detail of what I actually saw. An analogue download.

One day, maybe this loft will sit rotting and waiting for someone to clean it out and sell it to the highest bidder. I have pictures of me and Lisa all over this place. Any broker walking in here might convince themselves that at one time we were a happy couple. Look at us. There we were in Paris. There we were skiing. There we were on our honeymoon. We will mean nothing to them. Former owners long gone. Our images will be tossed out to depersonalize the space for prospective buyers. Eighteen hundred square feet of sanitized, tragedy-free potential happiness for a new owner who has no idea what happened in here.

I finish the sketch of my mother and caption it: *Why won't he leave me alone?*

It goes on the floor with the others. I step away from the vast landscape of work to get a wider view. Does that do anything for me?

No.

There's a broader sense of the scope to my vision, but the holes are immense. At best it tells me how much I don't know. A lot.

38

*It's two years ago.

I'm standing in the bathroom watching Lisa cry in the shower.

The room is filled with steam. The water is too hot for her to stay like that for as long as she is. It's got to burn but she's not reacting. She wants it to hurt.

She doesn't know I'm watching her. I can see her ribs through her skin like they were shrink-wrapped for sale in a butcher shop.

She spoke to her dad on the phone every night until she was twenty-five. She told me once that even when she was living with that moron hockey player she was so crazy about she still called her father every night. Just to touch base.

Her mother had preferred her younger brother. It's an open secret in the family. He's the favorite child. She spoiled him, really. In the most literal sense, she spoiled him. He started out the fresh, smart, handsome, young man with athletic ability boiling over. But couple that with an obsessive mother who loved to yell, but not really discipline, and nineteen short years later there he was in a rehab talking about his feelings and trying to blame everyone else for the mess that he was born to be. Consciously or not, she set him up to fail and spent his childhood making sure it would happen. Which left Lisa to bond with her dad.

He watched every soccer practice she ever went to. Helped with her homework nightly without fail. Drove her to sleep-away camp in Maine nine hours each way. Took her to Italy for her high school graduation. She used his credit card until she got her second job. He paid her rent until she made vice president. They still have lunch twice a month. He takes the train up to meet her.

I'm supposed to live up to that?

We spoke on the phone less than an hour ago and she sounded a little off but no more than usual since she got the news. It's been three weeks of roller coaster emotions. I've been wrong about everything. Anything that's not perfect is my fault. I'm a bottomless pit of responsibility. But that's my part to play. I'm replacing her father who took care of everything. Her shield. Only I'm terrible at it. I have no role models to reflect on. My moral compass is homemade and clunky. Not even sure it's magnetized. Asking me for emotional direction is like asking a couch for fashion advice.

She's so helpless, angry, spinning. There's nothing I can do. Or there's everything, but I won't do it.

I could ask how she's holding up.

I could tell her I'm coming home early.

I could listen.

I'm only good to a point and then I'm nothing. I don't know why.

If I had to bet, I'd say she's lost eleven pounds. She would say she's the same as she's always been and she eats plenty. And then she would smile and I would let that convince me to leave it alone. I'm pretty good at that.

He missed the diagnosis.

The brilliant doctor. The old family friend. The trusted oncologist. Thirty years in the business and he missed the diagnosis.

Missed it.

And I know Lisa. She's rehashing the scene she wasn't even there for over and over again in her head. Examining every possible angle in a futile effort to understand what happened. Asking questions no one can answer. Picking apart angles that no longer matter. Dealing with anything but the hardcore reality of the situation at hand. On some level, I know she finds the distraction comforting.

Were they too busy catching up? Trading stories about the old neighborhood? Planning their next vacation together? How do you miss something that obvious? It's your fucking job.

Of all people, a golfing buddy, the radiologist, called it. He stopped everything, right there on the green of the eighth and wanted to hear it all again but with more details. Then he called an oncologist he knew and asked for a favor.

Stage four. Metastasized to the brain and lymph nodes. Game over. They say her dad has six months to live. I give him three.

39

I got my first boner in jail.

Foster Mother drove me upstate to visit my father. He had been convicted six weeks earlier. He pled guilty, by the way. Guilty, guilty, guilty. Sentenced to life in prison instead of the death penalty for whatever lefty, liberal reason. I didn't go to the trial. Wasn't allowed to. I was told it would have been too traumatic. As opposed to what I saw at home? Doubtful, but the choice wasn't mine. So I hadn't seen him since he was taken away in a cruiser months earlier.

He had lost weight. And hair. Really, he looked terrible. Not that it was any of her business, but on the way home Foster Mother said that guilt can be a powerful thing. Ah ha. She never mentioned whom she had murdered so I'm not sure how she became such an expert on the subject.

The prison was minimum security. No fences or gates and I couldn't help overhearing another family remark repeatedly that it was a lovely (not their word) facility (not their word). This was in comparison to other prisons and/or jails in which they had visited loved ones. I couldn't help overhearing these comments because the lobby is all painted cinderblock and slick tile and nothing is quiet in there including their enthusiastic review of the place and the matriarch's amazement that she could wear a bra with an underwire past security. Metal detectors elsewhere usually caused her no small degree of aggravation but she had big tits so what are you going to do?

This I remember. Nothing from the night my mom died, but this stuff, this bullshit I overheard, is crystal clear.

My father was kept in a special section since he used to be a cop. That made him a target in prison. I don't think he was corrupt or anything but when you put a former policeman behind bars there are always plenty of inmates who want to kill him for whatever reason. Revenge. Initiation. Credibility. Thrills. The special section also usually houses pedophiles since they're not too popular either.

That's the crew you've got to spend the rest of your life with.

It would make me want to kill myself too. I never asked him if there were other cops in there or if it was just him and the kiddie rapers.

The wait to see him was about four hours. That's how they do you up there. Like you share some of the blame for the crime so you have to suffer. The inmates don't suffer. Not from the waiting. They're in jail. All they do is wait.

Visitors sit around and wait for hours with a bunch of other families they'd never otherwise spend time with. This on top of the fact that I didn't want to be there anyway no matter how lovely the facility was. I would have been happy to walk out at any time but Foster Mother thought it best for us to stay. I suspect there might have been a Child Care Services bonus awarded for a certain number of miles traveled or maybe she could see that Foster Father was beginning an angry, all-day binge that she didn't want to be around for. He got like that sometimes.

Oh, some days Foster Father was a real piece of work. Weeks would go by without a word from the guy and then something would set him off and we all had to listen to lectures on how to live our lives and what was wrong with America (me) and how things should have worked out differently for him. It was a tiresome drill but if you shut your yap and waited it usually ended soon enough. Or it would escalate into some good old-fashioned wife beating. But at least you knew that couldn't last forever. God, he was a bore. I suppose Foster Mother had lived with him long enough to see when the wind was changing for the worse before the storm actually hit. I think she borrowed the car from a neighbor.

What do you say to your father in jail?

How are you?

I hate you?

I love you?

Now what?

My friends had stopped talking to me after my mom died so I had no one to ask for advice. I became a ghost in the classrooms and invisible in the hallways. No one was particularly mean, per se. It was a matter of being ignored. I walked home alone. I studied alone. I stopped raising my hand. I stopped playing sports. Maybe it was me. Maybe I shut down. If I still knew any of those guys I would ask them. I wonder if they would remember me.

No one I knew had a relative in jail. Not a close relative, anyway. I had never heard about anyone's visits to their parent in prison. So I hadn't the slightest idea what to say and the stress was getting to me as I sat there and played with the ragged edges of the cheap plastic chairs in the lobby.

At this particular facility, they only fill the vending machines on Saturday. We were there on a Sunday, which meant the machines were empty because Saturday is a big day for visiting. Again, they don't make it easy on you. I was starving.

Would I be able to hug him? Would I if I could? Would he want me to? What if I tried and he backed off? He did put himself here away from all of us, after all. This was his decision alone. I hoped there was Plexiglas between us. I didn't want to make the choice. My heart raced like I had never experienced. I could feel the blood pumping through my chest. Sweating bullets.

And then I got an erection. A little-boy weenus erection, yes. But enough to make standing up uncomfortable at best and embarrassing at worst. I guess the racing blood had to go somewhere. I tried to think about baseball and math and anything to distract me from the stress that was engorging the stiff Vienna sausage in my pants. Nothing helped. I sat patiently and tried to wait it out, but a marble-mouthed jackhole in a green uniform walked out and called Foster Mother's name. She grabbed my arm and dragged me along behind, boner and all.

There was no Plexiglas.

My father hugged me and asked how I was before I had time to do anything. He was so glad to see me I got a little scared. He had always been such a powerful man and when I walked through that door, he melted. When I didn't answer him he started crying. He kept telling me how sorry he was and that he wanted me to understand it had to be this way. It was better for me. Better for everyone. And what could I say to that? Foster Mother sat in the background like a load and let me flounder around as I did not say things like *How is it better for Mom?* and *Well, thanks for executing this well-thought-out plan for my future, Dad* and *Why can't we go back to the way things were?*

—It's okay, Dad.

That's all I could muster. A watery pronouncement that everyone in the room knew was a blatant lie. What a coward. My father made himself calm down and smile and tell me he was doing 'great.' We spent the next hour talking about things that did not involve shootings or moms or police. At one point I noticed Foster Mother had nodded off. I told my father about the baseball team I was playing left field for and the girl I had a crush on and the book I was reading about robots that take over the world. All of which I made up.

Seeing him made everything worse. I didn't go back for years.

40

*It's a year and nine months ago.

I'm not hungry.

I already ate.

I'll eat later.

My stomach is upset.

I'm a vegan.

No, thanks. I'm allergic.

There are a million excuses for her not to eat, but these are the greatest hits. I hear them every day. Mostly she uses them to fend off the lunch and dinner offers of other people who are polite enough to pretend to believe her. She doesn't say them to me anymore. I've called her on it too much.

—I already ate.

—No you didn't.

—I'll eat later.

—No you won't.

—My stomach is upset.

—No it's not.

—Fuck off. I'm not eating.

She's killing herself.

Lisa's asleep in bed next to me. She always goes down before I do. Denial can be exhausting. Also, I think she likes the idea that I will take care of locking up and setting the coffee maker and turning off all the lights and whatever else has to be done. So do I. This is the routine that we have discovered works for us. We kill ourselves at work all day, meet up at home, and bore a hole in our heads with the predictable tropes of *Law & Order* while tamping down the rush of thoughts in our heads with our drugs of choice.

At some point the disease takes on a life of its own. It is an extra tenant in our apartment. The uninvited guest at every dinner we share together. It doesn't take much for the simple exercise of self-control to spiral into something so much worse. Coping mechanisms are insidious.

The sheets are crisp and the windows are cracked so wisps of the fall air can get in. I'm enjoying the last quarter of the double scotch I poured myself ten minutes ago. I can't sleep without it. She'll have a drink if it's the only option but prefers to self-medicate with weed. Either way, we both get where we're going. She just gets there sooner.

I suspect it's too late for me to help her without professional intervention. I barely have tools to maintain a relationship with her when she's not overwhelmed with guilt and anger. But this. It's beyond me. She's emaciated to the point of concern.

I watch her when she doesn't know I'm looking and she seems so empty and lost. Lisa is thirty-five but in these unguarded moments, all I see is a little girl I want to take care of but can't get close enough to. She's backed herself into a corner she doesn't have to be in. Her dad is going to die whether she starves herself or not.

Sometimes when she's desperate enough, she tries to talk to me but I don't have the facilities to manage that much raw emotion. Or I did but I used them all up selfishly on myself years ago. I nod and try to think of something to say that won't sound stupid or trite but it's usually both and she slams shut again.

I find myself confused by the storyline on the television and realize I've been nodding off for the last fifteen minutes. I finish the scotch on principal and move to turn the lights off when I see Lisa's sleeping with her glasses on. She really expects me to take care of everything.

I slip them off her face, fold them, and put them on her nightstand. In the process I stir her from the deep sleep she was already in. She furrows her brow and says something about me being an asshole but she doesn't fully wake up and I know she won't remember it tomorrow morning.

I lie back and turn my light off. I thought I would make a better adult.

41

—I need you to choke me.

Flaco misunderstands what I'm asking him to do because he barely speaks English which is infuriating and impressive at the same time. Fucking guy has been in America for twenty-whatever years from wherever he snuck in from and hasn't ever so much as stopped rolling his r's when he buys a lap dance.

I speak slower, as if that might help, and throw in some hand gestures.

—Not choke me like rough sex. I mean choke me until I pass out. And then a little bit more.

I need something less risky. Something predictable. Quantifiable. I can't keep hoping the ambulance gets to me in time. Plus I'll get committed if I keep it up. That's not my goal here. Maybe I can get the job done with the right amount of choking in the safety of my own home. Not enough to *kill me* kill me, but enough to get me back to The White long enough to nab another memory before Flaco slaps me awake or whatever. I wonder if he knows CPR. That would be such a bonus. If he doesn't, there's got to be a YouTube video for that. We'll look it up before we get down to business.

I thought about hiring a dominatrix who makes house calls, only I can't help but think whoever I find won't be entirely trustworthy. I feel like sex workers are usually in the industry for all the wrong reasons. Besides if she's any good at her job, the last thing she'll want to do is actually kill someone. Bad for business.

So I called Flaco.

He's got meaty hands like you'd want if your job was cracking walnuts for a living. Ham hands. From what I understand he grew up working with concrete. That'll do it. He could squeeze the life out of me with little to no effort. With that volume of muscle fiber, he should have a high degree of control. In theory.

Nuance is the key here. If he crushes my windpipe, I'm done. And from what I understand that only takes about fourteen pounds of pressure. Knowing how to apply pressure by degree is the secret. A dimmer switch as opposed to a toggle. I wonder if Flaco would understand that analogy. Probably not. I don't know that he's a nuance kind of guy.

Flaco finishes his beer, shakes his head, and mumbles some Spanish, most of which I don't get except the part where he calls me gay. He's disgusted but smells money so he stays.

You'd think he'd be used to odd requests like this. Flaco was our go-to scumbag when the firm needed some quasi-legal work done. Surveillance pictures. Dirt on an ex-husband. The address of a mistress. Shrooms. He was our guy. One time a colleague paid him to plant she-male porn on an opposing counsel's work laptop to ease the negotiation process. Even if he won't do it himself, he must know someone who can help me. Plus he knows how to keep quiet about what he sees.

I know as long as I'm buying, Flaco will sit here. I'll wear him down. I nod at the bartender for another round and tell him to keep them coming. I'm sure I can outdrink Flaco.

We sit and watch the game for another half an hour. Flaco manages to get three more beers and two shots into his fat belly before he finally loosens up.

—Five thousand.

Jesus, with that thick accent. I have to repeat his offer and clarify, because god forbid he elucidates on his own.

—Five thousand. You'll do it?

—No. *La Medica.*

His interpersonal skills are fucking terrible. What is he talking about?

—La Medica. Who's that? You got a guy who can help?

He shrugs and I think it means yes.

—La Medica es un . . . doc-tor.

A doctor.

Perfect. I knew Flaco would come through. Why hadn't I thought of approaching a doctor? People doctor-shop for prescription meds all the time. And these guys have to know they're dealing with addicts, right? What's the difference here? I'm not hurting anyone but myself and I stopped caring about that weeks ago. There must be doctors who need a little extra gambling cash and are willing to overlook a few minor details like laws and oaths. Flexibility. That's what I'm looking for. There's always a gray area. I need a doctor who doesn't mind practicing there.

—La Medica. She's bad. She's a bad person.

She? Really? I always pictured my bad doctors as either overconfident asshats with no conscience or quivering desperados with no choice. Always men, though. I feel like women are better than this. But apparently, they aren't.

—You know where she is? You have her number?

—We no can call. I show you.

Flaco has a body like a sack of bowling balls. He's not a big man, but he's solid. Dense. No way I could outwrestle him. It dawns on me now that I'm asking him to help me do something highly illegal and he's offering to take me somewhere I have to think is dark and on the other side of safe. I should be wary, but what's the worst that happens? He kills me?

—So, great. Let's go.

—Five thousand.

I patiently explain to Flaco that I don't have five thousand dollars. He seems to think that lawyers all make salaries in the five to ten million dollar range and walk around with pimp rolls. We go back and forth a few times before he finally settles for my fifty-inch flat screen and four Oxycontin. Harry would have been so proud.

—Let's go.

—Where are we going? Her office? It's ten o'clock at night.

—The dog fights.

42

*It's a year and nine months ago.

I'm standing in the kitchen arguing with Lisa about whether or not we even want to have kids after we officially get the word that her pregnancy test is negative. She got a positive reading from the test she bought at the drug store that guarantees it's 97 percent accurate and then went to the doctor to make sure. Turns out she was in the 3 percent.

We haven't had sex in five weeks.

I'm watching her talk and wondering why she can't finish a sentence but I'm not saying anything because it doesn't matter. She's so beautiful. Even more so when I'm angry.

She's stammering and justifying and explaining her position of waiting until the time is right and I don't care so I'm quiet while she rambles. With nothing to stem the stream of consciousness she's trying to pass off as a logical soliloquy, she tangents into more haranguing about the Vegas thing. I've got plenty to say about that but it's all been said before and she's so worked up there's no way she'd hear me. This is so much anger and avoidance, but what it is not is communication.

On the upside, the affair I'm convinced she's having has replaced her anorexia as her preferred means of distraction from her father's impending death. So there's that.

I wonder what would happen if I brought my open hand down really hard on top of my almost empty wine glass. Could I do it hard enough that the bowl would shatter and the stem would jam straight through my palm and out the back of my hand? It would have to be pretty forceful and there's a good chance of the stem running into a bone. I think the bones in your hand break easily, but probably not from wine glass stems. Still, I'm dying to find out.

We were supposed to be at the Grossmans' half an hour ago but she won't let go of the Vegas thing even though I know it's not really about the Vegas thing. I know she doesn't care about the Vegas thing because I overheard her annoying girlfriend ask her about it and I heard Lisa laugh. I don't say anything about her annoying girlfriend. Fucking hate Michelle.

I raise my hand to about the height at which I feel like I could generate the most velocity and hold it there. I could change the course of the evening in an instant if I brought it straight down. We could have a nice, intimate four-hour chat in the emergency room waiting area. I'm losing the buzz of emotion and severing a tendon won't get it back. Fuck it. I run my hand through my hair like I'm frustrated and then refill my wine glass. Funny how that can be appropriate in conversations like this. Civilized muggings that they are.

Fighting is the only way we connect lately so I jump back into the conversation and pile on with cheap shots and half truths to keep the conversation going. I love you so much, Lisa. Fuck the Grossmans.

43

Flaco keeps passing out on the train.

I shouldn't have given him the Oxy up front. I make him write the address out for me in case he nods off for good. Not that I know the Bronx at all.

What would Lisa think of this move? Probably not much. Too impulsive. I'd love to explain my reasoning to her, but I know I'll never get that chance. Not that she would listen.

I fall asleep for a few minutes and then jump awake when I'm convinced the train has run off a cliff and is plunging into a ravine. There are no cliffs in New York City. I'm so tired.

We get off at 183rd street. Flaco uses my shoulder more and more to keep himself upright. God damn he's heavy for a short guy.

I follow his slurry directions for forty-five minutes and we end up outside a twenty-four-hour grocery store that claims to have a wide selection of Mediterranean options. This is the address. It's almost midnight.

In my head I'm fighting with Lisa.

—Really? The Bronx? You fucking idiot. This neighborhood is one of the most dangerous parts of the city.

—What could happen?

—You could die.

—I've died twice this week. What else could happen?

It's quiet inside. Not a lot of twenty-four-hour shopping being done right now. The check out girl looks up from her texting to watch me like the sore thumb that I am. The homies in the back by the storage room entrance slide their heavily lidded eyeballs our way and then look to each other as we approach the door.

Flaco nods and waits for them to move. They don't. So we wait for them to speak. Apparently, this is the protocol.

—'Sup?

I don't even know Flaco's last name. We always paid him cash.

Flaco mumbles some garbled Spanish to the security detail and includes the words *La Medica*.

Silence. More quick looks.

The skinny one sighs and gives an almost imperceptible chin bob to indicate that we're cleared and the rest move enough for us to get by. As they slide back, I notice each has a handgun tucked under his shirt. Despite the Oxy, Flaco looks nervous.

44

(If you would indulge me for a moment.)

For those of you unfamiliar with the intricacies of dog fighting—and for the sake of decorum I will assume that encompasses the vast majority of you—a quick summary of the world our man has entered: It is fight night.

The fighters are dogs. The contests are brutal. This description is invariably and inarguably accurate. This is the fantastical microcosm the owners, bookies, and fans of dog fighting have created. A self-contained hell with its own bizarre rules and specific rituals agreed upon by the participants and rigorously enforced by the hosts. To the outsider, it is the shabby and primitive distraction of mean-spirited rubes. But to those involved, dog fighting is life.

The world is kept as secret as possible but, inevitably, reports from incidental or accidental eyewitnesses bleed out into the real world. Tales of unimaginable cruelty are whispered, with only the slightest tinge of pride, between shocked relatives. Posthumous horror stories of atrocities committed in the name of competitiveness are breathlessly related by on-the-spot reporters moments after a police raid. Regretful visitors explain their initial curiosity and eventual distaste for the sport to quasi-judgmental friends. Word spreads.

I heard they have a special stand they strap the prize female dogs to so the winning male studs can rape them to make super strong puppies.

I heard they electrocute the losers with a cut lamp cord and it can take up to ten shocks to kill them.

I heard they cut fighting dogs' ears off with wire cutters so there's nothing for an opponent to grab onto.

The stories are shameful enough that they are forcefully dispatched to the far recesses of memory as soon as the words are processed. Ignored to better pretend the world in which we live is not so hateful and cold. The natural byproduct of this collective contrived ignorance is the preservation of the layer of secrecy shrouding the sport. Who enjoys discussing such inhumanities?

The trainers do. Training regimens are endlessly refined and continuously optimized. Once it is determined that fighting dogs are of no value beyond their win/loss record and the winnings associated therein, there is no length to which the top competitors won't go.

The training of a fighting dog involves raising it from birth to adulthood restrained with heavy chains, and later additional weights, to build upper body strength. The dog is administered severe and frequent abuse to engender aggression and starved regularly to create severe hunger and profound desperation. They are made to tug on hanging objects to increase jaw strength and their teeth are filed to points to ensure the infliction of maximal damage to their equally sadistically trained opponents. Add to this a carefully calculated, protein-rich diet along with a generous helping of steroids and you end up with an animal composed almost entirely of angry muscles, razor sharp fangs, and mercenary attitude. A killing machine.

To prepare a dog for a fight, the combatants, usually bred for the sport, are beaten, baited, and made to spar with smaller, less dangerous animals including cats, rabbits, and smaller dogs who have been kidnapped from wherever convenient. Perhaps this is what happened to the faithful companion you left tied up outside the grocery store while you ran in for only a moment. If not yours, then thousands of others. A good trainer can go through a raft of live opponents in a week's time. The hope is that the regimen will spark a taste for fighting, blood, and killing as the dogs mature and grow stronger. It will become part of a fighting dog's DNA.

As you might suspect, but are trying to avoid lingering on, an event like this with more than a dozen of these very dangerous dogs must mean a great deal of bloodshed and mayhem and injury.

You are correct.

Dogs lose ears. Eyes. Blood. Legs.

The losers are destroyed immediately. No one likes a loser. But often the winners will sustain serious injury during a match and need immediate attention their owners lack the knowledge or ability to give them. Some need stitches. Some need broken limbs set to heal. Some need blood transfusions. Some need more than that. Whatever damage has been done will have to be repaired as soon as possible. Winners have to fight again, after all.

So they are taken to see La Medica.

45

Jesus fucking Christ.

These people are animals. The pit in the middle of the basement is about five feet deep and fifteen feet wide with a hundred frothing lower class gamblers crammed around it. You can smell the tension and the testosterone and the intensity.

The screaming. Men rabid in the throes of gambling. There must be ten thousand dollars in fives and tens exchanging hands as I walk by the ring. A pit bull is squaring off against a . . .

—What is that?

—Dogo Argentino. He will win.

Flaco knows fighting dogs. Not surprising.

I think of Lisa's lawyer. He won. I should have bet on him. I wonder how well he would do against the Dogo Argentino. Probably not bad.

—You come here a lot?

Flaco grunts and keeps walking back through the crowd of fat men sweating malt liquor and yelling, cheering, pleading at the dirt circle where the pit now has the Dogo by the neck.

From what I could get through Flaco's drugged up, third world English, La Medica owns the warehouse and hosts the fights. She's also the bank you bet against. More importantly, she's the doctor you see if you really want your dog to be a killer. And she's the one to see when you want it brought back from the dead. If you pay her enough and get your dead dog there fast enough, there's a good chance she can make that happen.

She sells and administers *las drogas*, which I understand to mean steroids, growth hormone, and the like. She also has some crazy expensive shit that she calls Angel Juice. The dogs who get injected with it fight like motherfuckers but are never the same afterwards. They say it's worth it.

Flaco talks to a couple of tough guys who shake him down for money that he gets from me. They send us deeper into the building.

In a back room that must be a garage, several large dog cages sit in front of tricked-out low riders and chromed-up SUVs. Each cage holds a dog bigger and more muscular than the next. The owners don't look twice at us, but the dogs watch our every move. Their eyes lit with hunger. They pace around in what little space they are allowed. I make eye contact with a black boxer mix. Those deep black pupils. Don't worry, buddy. We're both probably going to end up in the same place. Dead in an alley with nothing to show for it.

The further back we get, the fewer people there are and the quieter they get when Flaco asks them about La Medica.

One last dirtbag takes twenty bucks to let us go past to the back door. Flaco assures me she'll be easy to find. She's the only woman here. He won't go out the back door.

—I take you here. Now you go alone.

I go alone.

In the back parking lot. Fenced in. The gate is locked tight. The door behind me shuts and I hear the industrial lock being thrown. A group of men stand around the trunk of an old Cutlass sedan. Put a hibachi in between them and it would look like a contentious family barbecue. The sounds of a vicious dog fight are somewhere in the muffled distance. Presumably, this is the VIP area.

The men notice me come out, but don't give a shit. They're too busy arguing about something.

She stands in the shadows across the lot watching the men who have now begun to beat on the top of the trunk, yelling at it. La Medica has the type of features that look good in this kind of darkness. Angular. Efficient. Made to live on a diet of little to no light.

I approach her directly as I have no better ideas.

She turns her attention to me but doesn't change her position. She's completely in control. Waiting.

I slow to a stop as I get closer. She's short. That hair. Those eyebrows. She's not a dead ringer for Lisa, but in this light, fucking close. I remind myself that it's impossible. Lisa is not a crazy dog doctor. She gave to the ASPCA. I stop a good five feet away from La Medica.

—Flaco told me you could help me.

Her body is as lean and minimalist as her face. Nothing extra. Form following function perfectly.

I don't think she knows who Flaco is but he's the only point of reference I have in this world. I also don't think it matters. She looks through me like someone who has survived the last decade only by trusting her instincts. I know she already understands far more about me from this once-over than I intended to reveal. I want to take a step back toward the door I came out of more than anything in the world but I don't let myself. Finally, she speaks.

—You have a dog?

—No.

She waits like she has all night. What the hell am I doing here? I should walk away and try something else. But, what? I can't do it on my own. Flaco can do nothing else for me. There's nothing left.

—I need you to kill me.

La Medica looks me over.

—Who are you?

Who the fuck am I? To her I am nobody. A stranger asking her to perform an illegal act far worse than the illegal acts she is already involved with. And how did I get in here? She must have security. Someone must be watching me. How long until she snaps her fingers or nods to indicate that I should be removed from the premises with prejudice? What was I thinking? What argument could I possibly have to convince her to help me? I thought no further than getting access to her. I have no next steps laid out beyond standing here and hoping that my one last chance will come through for me. I am speechless. I am alone. I couldn't tell you where I am in the Bronx. I stand silently like the negligible human being that I am. She has beautiful blue eyes and a cast iron presence. I can't look away.

The muffled dog fight slows to a stop. The men stop yelling and listen. When they are satisfied the fight is over, they open the trunk of the Cutlass.

Half of them cheer and collect money from the dejected other half. One of the winners lifts a limp Rottweiler out of the trunk by its neck. It's bleeding profusely, one of its eyes hangs out of its socket, one of its ears torn almost completely off. The fur, skin, and muscles of its hind left leg have been chewed off to reveal bone.

The losers drag what looks like a dead Doberman (hard to tell with all the blood) out of the trunk and drop it to the ground. They yell to the good doctor and she finally blinks.

—Excuse me. I have to go to work.

She picks up her bag, hands me a card with a phone number, and walks away.

—If you're serious, call me.

When your father dies in prison, the letter they send you is one of four form letters. Your options are the letter they send when a death sentence execution has been carried out, the letter they send when someone dies of natural causes, the letter they send when someone is killed in prison, and the letter they send when someone kills themselves in prison.

I got the fourth. I was young enough and angry enough to accept that what they had written was true. My father had committed suicide by hanging himself from a washing machine in the laundry room. A washing machine! Technically it's possible. But, come on. As I got older, I began to realize that there was every chance in the world that the letter was bullshit. I can't imagine there was a full analysis of the circumstance under which this wife/mother murderer was found dead. No careful autopsy. No blue light sweep of the surrounding area. For all I know he was slumped up against the machine after a recreational gang rape/thrill kill and this was the easiest call to make.

For some reason the prison made it a point to include a return address positioned prominently in the top left corner of their letter. As if we might be engaging in some future correspondence. Potential pen pals.

The writing was as cold as a surgeon's scalpel.

To: Christian Franco

It is with deepest regret and heartfelt condolences that we must inform you of the death of your immediate kin, inmate #67L1019, Anthony Giacomo Franco. Inmate #67L1019 was found dead in the

Butler Correctional Facility inmate laundry facility at 19:34 on the night of October 20, 1991. As determined by a thorough investigation into the circumstances surrounding his death, Inmate #67L1019 created a makeshift noose using his pant legs and supported by the edge of his assigned washing machine. The cause of death has been officially ruled a suicide.

Inmate #67L1019 has been scheduled for cremation on October 27, 1991, unless specific instructions regarding alternative burial plans are received prior to that date.

The belongings of inmate #67L1019 have been catalogued and stored for pickup at your convenience. Belongings will be held four weeks before donation to a local charity. The balance of inmate #67L1019's canteen account minus administrative fees will be refunded to his next of kin via check to be mailed within 3–5 weeks.

Please direct any questions or concerns to Deputy Warden Cornelius Planto.

Cordially,
John G. Neal
Warden, Butler Correctional Facility

Cordially.

Like that softens the blow. Since then I want to vomit every time I see that word on a wedding invitation or a bris announcement.

Who knows what really happened. A cop in prison doesn't exactly have a long shelf life. I hadn't seen him in years. The letters he had initially sent stopped coming a long time before that and I had made myself stop caring. Thought I'd severed those nerve endings. I must not have done a very good job of it though, because when that letter showed up with the prison address on the front, my heart leaped. A fresh chance to start hating my father all over again. There's something so comforting about righteous indignation. I never showed Foster Mother the letter. Never mentioned it.

But I kept it.

47

I get there a little after nine the next night.

The apartment buzzer on the outside is labeled *Cordoba*. I feel like I should remember to Google that name along with the word malpractice when I get home. But I won't.

I left Flaco at the fights last night, bought a bottle of gin, and took a train home. I called the number on the card this afternoon when I woke up. She didn't answer and there was no machine. An hour later, I got a call from a blocked number. It was her giving me an address. I tried to ask how much cash I needed to bring but she hung up. So I brought everything I have and my watch. I'm sure it won't be enough.

Her office is amazing. You'd never guess from the Lower East Side shithole building that houses it. A three-floor walk up to get to her immaculate loft apartment, half of which has been converted to a mini hospital. The front room off the entryway is a large, high ceilinged room with a single couch facing one club chair. Nothing else. I'm on the couch. She won't sit. From my perspective, I can see what looks like an operating theater in the next room. Its walls are lined with equipment I can only guess about. No idea what it all does. A microscope. I recognize that. Refrigerators. A centrifuge. Surgical lights. Monitors. An operating table. The entrance hallway of the building smelled like dogs. I saw a stairwell to a basement. There were no names on any of the other apartment buzzers outside. I'd be surprised if Cordoba was her real name.

We make small talk about the fights for a few minutes. Me trying to get a feel for her. Her trying to determine how off-balance I am. It's the most bizarre first date ever.

The dog fighting world is fascinating to Cordoba from a sociological standpoint. Look at these men and how they live vicariously through their animals. As a society, we have evolved to the point that it's socially unacceptable for men to prove themselves by physically dominating rival tribes and clan members. But do it with a dog? In some circles, it's not only acceptable but encouraged, lauded and recognized as a practical substitute for hand-to-hand combat. It's manly.

Trunk fighting was Cordoba's idea. Her innovation to the sport. It was immediately embraced by a fringe group who self-selects to interact apart from the main stage. Generally there are only one to three trunk fights a night since there is no action to witness together as a belligerent crowd and that's the fun for most of the guys. Watching the bloodletting and ear rending and limb ripping. Taunting your fellow gamblers as the match momentum shifts back and forth. Screaming. But the hardest of hardcore gravitate to the trunks where it's win or lose and nobody knows anything until the trunk is popped open. For a certain type of gambler, that's the only rush big enough.

All of this she volunteers. I know she's waiting for me to show some sort of indication of judgment. I have none.

Instead, I sit watching her in awed silence. She's beautiful and in any other environment I would be attracted to her. There's too much other stuff going on here, though. First of all, she's got to be off her god damn rocker. She's composed, intelligent, and thoughtful but she hangs out at the dog fights, for the love of god. Doesn't have a dog in any of the fights but she's there every fight night. Organizing, supporting, reviving, bankrolling. And it can't only be about the money. She's bright enough to make a buck somewhere else if that was her concern. I suppose you could attribute it to a pure academic curiosity, but even that would be a lot to swallow. Curious or not, she must have a screw loose.

But that doesn't mean she can't do what I need her to do.

Yes, she has an insane fixation with dead and dying dogs. She loves her disgusting work. I saw those deep blue eyes light up when that Doberman hit the ground. Doesn't mean she's a bad doctor, though. I mean you can tell by talking to her that she's a different level of smart, and nuttiness always comes with that territory.

And then there's the lab. Wow. There's enough medical equipment in the next room that a spontaneous heart transplant could break out at any second. What happened in the weeks and months before I got here? Who was lying on that table an hour ago? Do I even want to know? What other stupid son of a bitch asked her for a favor before me? And more importantly, where is he now? Oy.

She looks less like Lisa in the light of this room, but I can't get the first impression out of my mind. Same body type. Similar mannerisms. Maybe I want to trust her so badly I'm projecting familiar characteristics onto her. She is going to kill me, after all.

Cordoba tells me she's a researcher by training and trade. The fights are her testing ground. She tries out the drugs she develops on the dogs of unsuspecting clients. She'd rather it was people, but when something goes horribly wrong with a person, there's a lot of explaining to do. If your subject survives, they're living, breathing proof of your activities and a witness who might testify against you. If they die, you've got to do something with the body, which, believe it or not, is no simple matter in New York City. With a dog, live or die, you put them down and move on. Nobody asks questions about a dead dog.

Good to know.

At some point she's sussed me enough to get to the meat of the matter.

—To be clear, you want me to medically induce death in a reasonably healthy patient and then immediately reverse the process?

—Yes. Kill me and bring me back.

—Why?

—I'm looking for something. It's the only way I can find it.

—What are you looking for?

—Memories.

Hard to tell if she understands what I'm doing or sees me as a freebie—a willing subject that no one would miss if it doesn't work out. It's clear I don't have a lot going on and who with any family or friends would be in this situation? She said it was hard to get rid of a body in New York City. But she didn't say it was impossible.

She looks me over in silence for a minute. I don't think it mattered how I answered the last questions. I could have said I was looking for the fountain of youth or the perfect nap and she would have nodded just the same. The temptation of having a specimen like me walk in unsolicited and beg her to do what I'm asking must be tremendous. I'm not some homeless carbuncle who's three steps from dying anyway and will fuck up any anesthesia she uses with dope-saturated blood. I'm alone, fit, and eager. Jackpot.

—When was the last time you died?

—I'm not crazy.

I'm quite sure the tone of what I'm saying is more convincing than the actual words. I could be speaking in tongues, but as long as I remain calm she'll take me seriously.

—When?

—Two days ago.

Her eyes narrow the slightest bit as she processes this. She finds me intriguing. It's been a long time since anyone thought I was intriguing.

—I'm ready to go again. I need to.

Cordoba nods and allows herself the most modest of smiles. Like she's heard this before. Like she's heard a guy tell her he died forty-eight hours ago and is jonesing to hop back in that saddle. No way that can be true, but there she is. Could be worse. Who wants to go to a doctor that lacks confidence?

—You need to recover.

She digs around in a refrigerator full of hand-labeled bottles. Hands me a syringe and a vial of clear liquid.

—You okay with needles?

At this point, what am I not okay with? I nod.

—Find a vein. Take it all. Come back when it wears off.

—How long will that be?

—Two days. You'll sleep most of the time.

—What is it?

—It's homemade. You wouldn't believe me if I told you. But it helps.

I pocket the drugs. What the fuck? I've lost so much weight in the last few months, finding a vein will be easy. And, honestly, I wouldn't mind sleeping for two days.

—I can't pay you.

—Yes you can.

She walks to the front door and opens it, inviting me to leave immediately.

—Go. Heal.

48

*It's a year and a half ago.

I'm having lunch with a man I think of as a friend.

He's one of those guys who I feel a bond with but I can never tell how strong. We've spent a lot of time together socially, but I don't know where he grew up or if he has a brother.

Close or not, I have trouble knowing what's appropriate to share or hide or joke about with people with whom I share this vague intimacy. That includes the majority of people I would classify as friends. I never know what to say so I stick to sports or drink a lot or shut the fuck up and listen. Today I've tried talking baseball and pop culture bullshit, but this guy came here with an agenda. Apparently, he felt it was perfectly appropriate to ruin my day by dumping his personal problems on me in the middle of what is undeniably a loud restaurant.

He's telling me about his wife. I know her as well. She's smart and funny and when we go out as two couples we all get along. I'd fuck her if I were single, but I'm not so I settle for witty banter and clever one-upmanship. At dinner, sometimes we sit with the men across from each other so they can chat. Sometimes it's the guys across from the women. It always seems to work out, though. As I recall, she's a former teacher and current housewife. I always think she would have made a good lawyer.

He tells me they're having trouble. His wife doesn't respect him. Treats him like an assistant. A rented mule on which she can pile her troubles regardless of the strain to his back. An asshole. He claims to have had enough and if it weren't for their kids (He has kids! Who knew?), he would have been divorced months ago. In other words, he would stand up for himself but he doesn't have the sack. Their sex life is dead. They haven't slept together since last Christmas. We've had dinner with them four times since then.

Not only can I not identify with any of this, but I find it irritating. Why are they wasting our time as a couple pretending everything is okay when divorce is the inevitable end result of all this fretting and hand wringing? I listen and I nod and I ask a question or two to maintain a facade of interest but I still don't have the foggiest with regard to how much to commiserate or share or even to lie. What do other men do? How would guys I look up to react in this situation? How about the confident ones who intimidate me so easily with their natural charm and innate social skills? What would they do in my seat? Is this where I open up and talk about some common ground of misery? Is this where I tell him that inside I'm rotted and empty? I'm a human sinkhole waiting to collapse. I have it worse than you, Bub. Does that make you feel better? What do I share? I stand at the edge of the train platform sometimes and think *Who would care?*

How much is too much? Is he telling me this to get me to open up about my marriage? How could he possibly know what goes on in my home? He's not that clever, and I've never told anyone. Does he really expect me to start now? Here, over the Cobb salad? And why would I pick him of all people? We're not even that close. How do I know him? I can't remember how we met. A friend of a friend? Is anything he's telling me even real? I wonder if he's making it up. Bait. Maybe. We have such a good time together as a foursome. I'm exhausted.

—What a bitch.

I didn't know what else to say. I know he's taking it as a statement of support, but I'm really talking about him.

He starts crying. Not real crying. The kind where his eyes well up and he catches himself and smiles like he's embarrassed and now we have this little shared moment that I hope I can forget as soon as possible. In his mind we just became closer and this will lead to more chats like this.

He tells me that no, she's not that bad and she has her good side and it's not fair to talk about her like this when she's not here to defend herself. I feel like that's the best time to talk about her. If only he could do it with someone else.

I'm quiet and hope that my distaste is mistaken for sympathy or empathy or who gives a shit what it's taken for. By the time I finish the thought I'm livid. So angry I can't see straight. I excuse myself and walk past the bathroom out the front door without telling Captain I-don't-appreciate-what-I-have I'm leaving. He's lucky I don't punch his crybaby face.

I know I'll never talk to that guy (the bitch) again. But then, I kind of knew that as soon as he started complaining about his reasonably attractive wife.

Later, I have a massive fight with Lisa but I forget what it was about.

49

I hate needles.

This one is shiny and sterile and razor sharp and I take a long look at it after removing it from its packaging. The tip is cut at an acute angle to make the finest point possible. It should go in so easily. Cut straight through my dirty skin.

I jam it through the rubber on the vial and fill the syringe. Tap the air bubbles out and gently push the plunger up. Pretty sure I got them all. Close enough.

I should clean my arm before I inject myself but I don't.

Two days ago I was dead.

A few glistening drops slide down the needle. Taunting me.

What are you looking at, chump?

The drops are odorless. I have no idea what I'm putting in my body.

Rat poison.

Saline.

Angel Juice.

I don't know.

Fuck it.

I'm lean. I've got good veins that are helped out by the belt wrapped tightly around my left bicep. They look like a road map. A guide I might use to escape myself. I pump my fist a few times and insert the needle into the winner on my forearm. I'm an easy stick and the needle is so god damn sharp it slides in like it wants to be there. Look at this plastic and metal technology sticking out of me. I can't be helped any other way.

It's come to this.

Three weeks ago I was a practicing attorney.

I pull the plunger back a little to suck some my own blood out of my body to mix with whatever I've already got in the syringe. I saw it in a movie about drug addicts.

Lisa would say I'm an idiot.

—A 'doctor' you met at the dog fights?

—They say she's the best.

—Oh, well, *They* say so, huh? *They* being the disgusting child molesters who would have also been perfectly willing to recommend a good sex slave dealer? Well, as long as *They* recommended her. That's as good as five stars on Yelp.

—I'm a deep, dark hole of black ashes without you.

Two years ago I was a rising star.

—She probably made that stuff in her bathtub. You don't know if it's sterile or spoiled or stale or expired.

—It's not. Or it is. What else am I going to do?

—Not this. Don't do it.

—You never called back. Not once.

A year ago I was married to the love of my life.

I do it.

I ease the plunger down and force everything into my vein. It hurts a lot. And then it doesn't. I get the belt off my bicep before I lose all motor control. Didn't get the syringe out of my vein. Too late now.

I wonder if I should have left a note.

Black.

Black.

Black.

I remember drinking a gallon of water at one point. I remember yelling.

Beyond that I was immersed in a velvety pool of dense nothingness that smothered my psyche and held everything that was me down, down, down so whatever needed to happen could happen. I had no dreams. I had no nightmares. I had no thoughts. I was awake and then I was asleep and now I am awake. I was not awake when I chugged the water. I was an empty robot. A drooling zombie. A motile humanoid with no conscience or will power. Just id and thirst. When I yelled it was nonsense. Passionate nonsense informed by nothing and fueled by empty anger. Yelling in tongues. I remember staring at the exposed brick wall in my apartment for what must have been an hour. Focused. But I was not awake. Whatever needed to happen has happened.

I wake up in a pool of sweat and shit and piss and vomit. I've lost ten pounds. My nails have grown half a centimeter. It's daytime. I'm in my bathroom. The mirror is broken. The syringe is in the sink.

I've got a healthy crop of stubble on my face. More than I should for the time that has passed. But I look much better than I did before the shot. Less sallow. Less dead.

I've been out for thirty-six hours.

I shower and drink another gallon of water and realize I feel fantastic. I could run a marathon. I could lift a car. I could smile.

The rat poison/saline/angel juice worked. Who knows what kind of toll it took on my liver to get me here. I don't care.

As I said, this is not a long-term strategy.

50

(Well, well, well.)

Our man has thus begun his master plan.

The calculated, and now medically assisted, death and rebirth of a man no one would miss. The selfish inquisition into a life history best left untouched. The archaeological reincarnation of a nobody. Ridiculous, yes?

No matter. He is of a single mind and dogged in his pursuit. Even more so, now that he has the unabridged support wrought from his new partnership with a mind so brilliant in matters of medicine and so open with regard to medical ethics. The good doctor. The stealthy resident of the Hippocratic fringe who now soaks in the spotlight on the center stage of the old boy's world. She is his new lease on life. She is the Watson to his Crick. The orange juice concentrate to his gasoline. They are complementary. Synergistic. Volcanic. Or so go his rambling bloviations, the manic projections of our man and his omnium-gatherum of ill-conceived twaddle.

As the old boy sits in this grimy diner eating his third full breakfast of the morning, he visualizes the immediate future and the tantalizing possibilities contained therein.

More death.

More memories.

More answers.

It's intoxicating. His only concern is making sure to retain the good doctor's attention and stoke her zeal for the project. She is shining bright with enthusiasm for the moment, but white star zeal has a tendency to burn intensely and then not at all. There may be no time to waste.

The odd sensation in the back of his head he will attribute to anticipation. Hope. Relief. He believes he feels the deep satisfaction of a meaningful connection. The long awaited access to untapped potential. This is the thrill of being on the verge of something great.

Had he questioned even the slightest bit deeper, perhaps he might understand the feeling to be less of an emotion and more of a warning. As if he was in danger. At risk.

As if he was being watched.

But by whom? The tired-out waitress? The decrepit Hispanic gentleman lingering over his free refills of bitter, bitter coffee? The mustachioed gentleman reading the sports pages with his back to us? Who would possibly be taking note of the old boy, cracked and corroded with his inwardly focused fascination? To put it in words our man might use himself, Who would give a shit?

Looking back one day, he might wonder why it wasn't more obvious to him.

51

Fucking starving.

The waitress doesn't blink when I order enough food to feed a boot camp. This isn't the kind of restaurant where the employees are paid enough to give a shit about anything. I feel bad about planning to stiff her, but I don't have much of a choice. I have to eat and fucking Flaco spent most of my cash getting me to Cordoba.

Cordoba.

She's definitely passed the first test. I'm back in action without so much as a headache. She's crazier than a shithouse rat, but she does cook up some powerful drugs.

The place is almost empty. It's eleven in the morning. The waitress works the tables and I can hear a short order cook in the back. There's an old guy at the counter nursing a coffee. A guy at the table next to me reads the paper. He's facing away, but when he turns the pages I can see headlines about a financial crisis or a war or something.

My mind is empty. Cleared out by whatever I went through. The magic syringe. The endless black. A magnificent purge. I try to relax and pay attention to nothing. I want no distractions or miscellaneous information clinging and clogging up my now pristine mental facilities.

I slam the food down as fast as I can. Suck down another cup of coffee and I am ready.

I asked for my check a few minutes ago. To make it look legit. I wait until the waitress clears Newspaper Guy's plates to stand up. When she heads back into the kitchen to dump the dishes, I walk out the side door I sat next to knowing I would be skipping.

No way the waitress could have caught up to me but the whole way home I feel like I'm being followed. I keep checking even though I know that if she found me there's not a god damn thing she could do. She couldn't even prove I was in her diner.

Cordoba told me it would be two days. I think I know why. My guts are churning as my body puts the food to work rebuilding me. Every ounce of energy I have is getting co-opted into the process. I'm fading fast. I need to lie down.

I keep checking but there's nothing over my shoulders. Nobody racing to find me. Just the usual flotsam of city people bustling about with whatever they're so busy with instead of paying attention to the breakfast thief.

Feels like someone's there though.

I go back to my apartment and sleep for nineteen hours.

52

*It's a year and eight months ago.

She's not answering my very simple question.

Or perhaps that's the answer in itself. None of your god damn business.

The little black Japanese character is such a brazen statement. It's tiny and I'm not even sure how long it has taken me to notice it. It could have been there for weeks. Regardless of the timing, she won't tell me what it means. Brushes me off like I'm trying to sell her something she already owns four of.

—It's just a fun thing I did with Michelle.

Fucking hate Michelle. I always have. She's baggage from Lisa's past life and I know she doesn't like me. I've never heard her say it, but my gut tells me so every time we're in the same room. Not like a whisper in my ear that says *Ooh, I think something's up with that girl.* More like a radio broadcast. A morning zoo DJ laughing at his inside information about Michelle's feelings for me. And how they talk about me. And the lies she tells.

Michelle would say anything to cover for Lisa. She'd probably go get the same tattoo if it would make Lisa's story more believable. Which it wouldn't. Michelle is always the cover. Always the alibi.

I'm having lunch with Michelle.

I'm going to the movies with Michelle.

It's girls' night out.

I think it's the same guy I almost found out about before. Which would make him a boyfriend. My wife has a boyfriend. Awesome. You know he talked her into getting the tattoo. Pissing on his territory, no doubt. Not man enough to face me openly, but clingy enough to leave his mark. Wuss.

Michelle probably set them up in the first place and gave them a key to her apartment. I bet she changes the sheets for them when they're done. If she were watching this little scene play out, she'd work that cunty smirk of hers and shake her head the tiniest possible bit, but I'd see it. Fucking hate Michelle.

From what I can tell through my online research, the tattooed character means 'Life' in Japanese. Life.

So what does that translate to in Lisa's mind?

I'm celebrating life with a tattoo on my hip?

I'm serving a life sentence?

I'm memorializing my father so he's always with me?

I thought it was a pretty design?

I know what it means to me.

53

Why she feels it's important to have her degrees on the wall, I don't know. It's not like she's practicing legal medicine. Yale undergrad. Harvard Medical School. MIT. PhD. Who could she possibly be trying to impress? Herself? No way she has an actual practice. Could there really be a regular crowd of patients funneling through here? People desperate for alternative care who need the reassuring approval of big-name universities? The degrees look real, anyway.

The operating table I'm lying on is human size. There are restraints hanging from the side. Six full syringes lie neatly in a row on the tray to my left. Next to the syringes are scalpels and clamps and other frighteningly specific tools I don't want to know about. That's her business. What I do want to know is how the fuck she got here. Not this office, but this station in life. Nobody gets to this dark place without something going horribly wrong. Why the underground practice? Can't just be a love of dogs. Certainly not the company.

—So what happened?

She answers like she's bored of hearing herself explain her situation over and over. Like this question gets asked a lot. As if the answer is one that any number of people would give were they asked. Like it's not wildly unusual. Meanwhile, I'm one of what can't be more than five people in the world who have asked it. No way she makes small talk with strangers. No way she has friends. Maybe she's bored with life.

—Stripped of my medical license for practicing advanced experimental psychiatric research outside of government regulation. And some other stuff.

All of the degrees bear the name, Cordoba. First name, Isabel. I wish I didn't know that. She's becoming a person to me. I liked her better as an ideal.

—And now?

She indicates to the operating theater around us. We're in the back room of her loft. More machines. Monitors. Video cameras. The gleaming white of sterile surfaces. The doors on the refrigerators in this room have keypad locks on them. There's a gun on the counter.

—And now I don't have the patience to wait for modern medicine to catch up to my ideas. So I'm moving forward on my own.

I nod. The philosophical rationalization of dangerous medicine. Okay. Fine.

—Everything here is state of the art. Some of it is so cutting edge hospitals and research centers don't even have it yet.

—They can't afford it?

—They don't know about it. I made it myself.

Uh huh. She might be more arrogant than I am. Harry would have referred to that as a fatal flaw. I like to think of it as a valuable tool. Armor.

—Have you done this before?

—Yes.

—Seriously?

—Let's call it a hobby.

Let's.

—With who?

—There are people who will let you do anything to them if you pay them enough.

—How much is enough?

—Usually twenty dollars and some meth.

Ah.

—Before we get started, any medical conditions I should know about? Allergies? Conditions? Diseases?

—No allergies. No conditions. I had some minor STDs in college. But who didn't?

She nods and makes a note as she answers.

—Me. Anything else?

—No.

I'm shirtless. Lying on the table. The IV feeders inserted into the pronounced veins that line the gristle of my arms await syringes. My chest is riddled with patches connected to wires leading to monitors. The machines beep behind us. I feel like there should be a nurse or technician helping out here. Is she really going to do this whole thing herself? What if something goes wrong? What if she has a heart attack in the middle of the procedure? What if no one knows I'm here and I die and that's it? We'd both be powdered bones before anyone would think to look for us. There is no safety net.

Why is that exciting?

She pulls a restraint up and starts strapping me in. Right wrist first. This, I didn't expect.

—Ahh . . .

My hesitation is clear, but she doesn't pause in the slightest. If anything, she speeds up.

—You may have some spasms.

—How exactly does this work?

She yanks the restraint tight. I may never get out.

—It's basically an overdose. But with a time-released, counteracting antidote. A toxic screener slash blood cleaner.

Ah. The old toxic screener slash blood cleaner trick.

—So, no surgery?

I eyeball the scalpels. Maybe I care a little bit.

—Not for what you want. I take you down. I bring you up. It's all needles.

She straps in my left wrist. I'm helpless.

—And we may have to use the paddles and some adrenaline.

—An overdose on what?

She straps in my right ankle. She pulls it tighter than it should be but I say nothing. How many times have I hurt myself and blown it off with the phrase 'I'll live'? I'm tempted to use that here but I know it might not be true.

—Synthetic heroine.

—Is that the 'other stuff' that you got in trouble for?

She straps in my left ankle.

—No.

She fastens a strap snugly across my waist and pats my chest.

—So, ready to die?

I nod. Yes. I'm ready to die.

I am ready to die.

Cordoba looks over her arrangement of needles. A spark of intensity in her eyes. This is the good part. She practically drools.

She picks a syringe up and taps the air out of it.

—We'll start fairly slow and then escalate.

She inserts the needle into one of my IV feeders. Gently guides the plunger in.

I've never done heroin. Not once. I was always more of a cocaine guy. Lisa told me she tried heroin once in college. Thought it was coke and snorted a rail. She liked, but didn't love. It was probably shitty heroin.

—How do you feel?

—Fine.

She waits.

Holy shit.

My eyes suddenly droop.

—I . . . whoa.

—How about now?

My lips move, but I can't speak. I can see the doctor and I love her more than anything in the world. Maybe I am a heroin guy.

—Christian. Focus.

I can see what barely registers as excitement in the good doctor's eyes as she taps the air out of a second syringe and inserts it in the other IV feeder.

Yes. More please.

She waits a beat and then slides the plunger down.

—Christian?

My eyes are still open, but I can't respond.

The heart monitor's beeping slows.

She's so fucking excited she can barely take her eyes off of my face to check it.

She grabs a third needle, taps the air out, and inserts it.

This time she watches my face as she plunges the third syringe.

The monitors slow even further. Warning alarms blare from at least two of the machines.

She slides her hand down her skirt.

Oh.

She's masturbating.

I know something's off here but I'm losing touch so fast I can't form a clear thought beyond that one.

I'm fading into somewhere.

Unconsciousness.

Heaven.

Myself.

With her free hand she inserts a fourth syringe and jams the plunger in quickly. Much faster than the other three.

My eyes loll around my head independently of each other. As my right eye swirls I see her check the monitors. I can hear them quickly slow to almost nothing.

Perfect.

She leans in and tongue kisses me.

I flatline.

Black.

54

White.

Silence.

I'm naked and formless and completely aware that I'm in The White. I am content.

Waiting.

If nothing happened, I'd be okay with that too. I have no worries here. No mortgage, no job, I don't even have to shower. No pain, no happiness, no hope, no despair. I'm even. So even I never want to leave.

And then I hear the whoosh. Maybe I do want something to happen. I know the memories are coming and I have to force myself out of the comfort zone The White floods me with. Get ready. You only have so long. Concentrate. It's worth it.

Memories fly by. Zillions of them in an angry flurry. To my side. Below me. Above. How the fuck am I supposed to find anything in this place?

I strain to slow them down. Work to focus on what I'm seeing.

There goes an awkward office party. That asshat Brennan mouthing off about his bonus when he's the laziest bastard we ever hired. Me typing a brief on that awful old computer. Buying lunch across the street from my office.

There I am haggling with a car salesman before walking out.

There I am brushing my teeth.

Doing laundry.

Washing the dishes.
Waiting for the subway.
Calling a client.
Taking notes.
Painting a wall.
Yelling for Warren Haynes to play *Soulshine*.
Finding a parking ticket.
Unlocking a door.
Rolling up a sleeping bag.
Walking through a mall.
Running. Fixing a faucet. Tipping a sommelier.
This is crazy.
Organizing my e-mails.
Pledging that dumb frat.
Punching a doorman.
Downloading Carolla.
Ordering lamb chops.
Downloading music.
Working out with a trainer.
Checking my voicemail.
Plumbing my drain. Shaving. Shifting into third.
This is a waste.
No. It's not.
There. A memory from my ninth year.
I will it closer. Am I flying toward it or is it flying toward me?
The memory hits me square in the face and I'm there.
Brooklyn.
My home.
I'm eight.
My stupid little eight-year-old brain is on fire.
Yelling. My father and mother are screaming at each other in the kitchen. I'm in the next room watching. From the feel of it, they've been fighting for weeks. The tension. My god. I'm feeling the persistent taut uneasiness that used to live with us every day. It's right there with me.

Saturating the room. I'm not shocked or surprised at what I'm seeing. I'm used to it. My father is furious. My mother is scared. I've never seen her like this. Or maybe I have. But only lately. Things have been getting worse. He's so much louder than her.

—I've had enough of your shit!

—Stop trying to control me!

My mother's white knuckled fingers are locked onto her purse. I want them to stop, but I know they won't. I want to run and hide but I don't. I'm frozen with fear and what I now understand to be fascination. How can people treat each other like this? Is this the way things are supposed to be? This what adults do? Is this happening in our neighbors' houses? Will I be this angry when I'm bigger? About what?

I'm trembling.

My father grabs the purse and fights to pull it out of her hands. He may be more intense than she is. I know this is the first time their fights have gotten this physical. I know my mother won't talk to me tonight. I know I'll put myself to bed. I know I will lie awake most of the night listening to her wail and cry. I know that soon my father will disappear for days. I know I'll wonder if this is my fault.

My father shouts.

—I want that money!

—No!

My sister is behind me. I look at her face. She's terrified. Quiet tears run down her cheeks. She wants me to hold her and make it go away. I'm older and sometimes I tell her I'll take care of her. I know it makes her feel better so I tell her this when we're alone in my bedroom or hiding in the basement. She crying so hard she's shaking but she won't make a sound because we both know that will make things much worse. I don't say anything to her or hold her. I can't. If I do I'll collapse. I stare at her and do nothing. I'm eight. She's three.

I turn back to my fighting parents.

—I am done fucking around! Give it to me!

My father smacks her hard across the face and yanks the purse out of her hands, knocking my mother down in the process. She's bleeding from her mouth. Her eye is already swelling. She crawls after him, trying to grab it back. Struggling. Savage.

—NOOOO!

My father shoves her away, yanks out her wallet, and takes all the cash and credit cards. He drops the purse and heads for the back door.

She collapses.

—What about my medicine?!

She curls up in the corner and howls. I turn to see that Ella has run to her room to do the same.

I'm eight. She's three.

I try to suck all this in and more. Every emotion. Every physical detail. Every word spoken. The setting. The time. The wallet. My father's voice. My mother's tears. This room. What does it smell like? What's on the counters? Where did he go? I want to know it all but the scene is fading fast. The colors are washing out faster than I can absorb them.

I see the ghost of my father turn toward me and open his mouth to speak. But the sound in the memory was the first thing to go so I can't hear what he's saying and soon it doesn't matter because the color is gone and I'm left with nothing.

Black.

55

(And there he is.)

The old boy, lying there unconscious as if he hadn't a care in the world. Tucked into a hospital-grade patient bed, mere hours past his latest, carefully choreographed, near-death experience, he has slipped back into the sound, if medically assisted, slumber of a newborn baby. A propofol nap. Had we not already thoroughly acquainted ourselves with him, it might be tempting to refer to his as the sleep of the innocent. But, that would be an unnecessary injection of ironic hilarity in an otherwise serious situation.

While by no means innocent, our man is decidedly unaware of the machinations of the good doctor who is performing mere inches from his practically lifeless body.

She's quite busy proving herself to be the talented and dedicated physician the old boy believed her to be, providing service far and above what one might find in a traditional hospital. She's patient and caring and a careful note taker. She's observant, anticipatory, and methodical. In short she is precisely what he needed. Not that our man deserves it. But, what luck indeed.

Monitors are checked. Responses are measured. Meters are watched. Lady Cordoba remains patiently at his side until she has established our man is recovered enough for the second stage of her plan.

Ah ha.

It would appear that she is not only a skilled emergency doctor and a brazen, if ethically barren, medical researcher, but also a gifted surgeon willing to act unabashedly alone where others would insist on a team of medical experts as a matter of support. Unprofessional? Without a doubt. Adept and impressive? Indubitably.

And on top of all of this, she is a brilliant businesswoman.

Observe her haggling tooth and nail, even as she works, with the Asian gentleman who has recently joined us. He is without question a shark, and, while my Korean is a tad spotty, it's clear to see the good doctor is not readily amenable to lowering her substantial fee. The Korean inveigles and cajoles and whines and threatens, but she remains the unemotional counterpart to his screaming attempts at chicanery, palaver, and intimidation, a masterful strategy on her part. Inevitably, the Korean overplays his gambit, and when both parties understand he is without leverage beyond financial resources, he buckles and agrees to her original asking price. After forcibly regaining his composure, the Korean leaves Cordoba to administer her patient care as if he had never been there.

Hours later, the Korean returns with an elegant attaché. When he presents its contents, Cordoba deigns to look only as long as is necessary to confirm that he has proffered a small velvet bag of diamonds, as promised. Curt nods are exchanged, the case left on a counter, and the Korean is instructed to wait in the front room. Cordoba continues her bloody, bloody work.

There is much to do.

56

I open my eyes to find Cordoba standing over me.

She did it. I'm alive.

She says something that I think is a question. Or a warning. Or an apology. I haven't the slightest idea.

She's so beautiful and I love her for this gift she has given me. I want to hug her but my arms won't move. I want to thank her, but my eyes are closing at the thought. She has opened my heart or my mind or wherever I have been storing all these memories and without her I would have never found them and it's not too late to make up for lost time and we should talk about this. Just us without so many meddling friends. I want to tell her how much she means to me and that we should never be apart and it's all a big mistake that we should have worked harder to avoid. Everything I realized I should have told her before it was too late. I feel like this is a miracle and we shouldn't waste it. I want to promise to not take too much of her time. Maybe we could sit quietly and hold hands and look at each other because sometimes that's enough. I want to say her name.

I think there's a tube in my throat.

I try to speak but the effort is overwhelming.

Black.

57

*It's a year and three months ago.

I'm sitting in my office pretending to work late but really just drinking.

In the last week or so, I've begun to notice that if I'm alone for a long enough stretch of time, I have suicidal thoughts. Not suicidal intentions. These are different. Suicidal thoughts.

Not *Ooh, where's that gun? I sure would like to kill myself right now.* More like philosophical ruminations of how much easier it would be if I swallowed some Drano or fell asleep in my garage with the car running. Easier than trying to explain myself to Lisa or figuring out what the correct response to increasingly bad news about her father is. I know I should at least respond in some way. I look at her and I know I should do something.

Do some thing.

She's leaning on me. Counting on my emotional help. Whether she realizes it or not, she's begging me with her actions to work my arms free of the psychological ties that bind them to my body. Catch me, Christian.

I realize it, but I let her fall right through me anyway. My support an ethereal tangle of confused emotions I should have dealt with long ago. I don't know what's in the dark cloud that has supplanted sympathy on my part. I should figure that out. Do some soul searching. Hold her.

But I don't. And even though I do nothing, even though my cruel, cruel behavior burns exactly zero calories, somehow I know that erasing myself from the planet would be easier.

I don't have a car or a garage and I know I would hate the taste of Drano. Also, I can't see myself actually going through with it. I'm a narcissist and as much as I hate my very being, I hold myself, at the same time, far too important to commit suicide.

But still, the logic is there. I could make things so easy for everyone concerned.

I'm not sure these are what a licensed psychiatrist would officially classify as suicidal thoughts. I'm only guessing they are what the calming voice at the end of pharmaceutical commercials refers to while we all watch someone catch butterflies or throw a football through a hanging tire or drift comfortably off to sleep.

If you're having suicidal thoughts, discontinue use and consult your doctor.

The thinking being that suicidal thoughts lead to suicidal intentions.

58

*It's a year and two months ago.

We're driving back from her dad's funeral and she hasn't cried yet.

Not for weeks. She won't talk to me about her father. I stood with her at the funeral but she wasn't there. Didn't say a word the entire service.

We get home and Lisa walks away before we get to the front of our building. She just leaves. Walks up the block. I don't call after her because I know she won't answer.

Her father left her a bunch of money, his watch collection, and a letter Lisa won't read. She sat with him for the last three days before he died. I don't think she slept for the last two. She was in the room when he died and I know that meant a lot to her. I was at work.

She walks up the block and turns the corner without looking back.

I go up into our apartment and sit on the couch. I don't make myself a nice tall scotch and sit there and drink it. I don't chug vodka straight from the bottle. I don't pour a carafe of red wine down my throat. I sit on the couch and think nothing.

My dry cleaning lies on the bed still in its plastic wrapping. I let it slide to the floor when I get in bed an hour later. I'm so tired I can't think. Sleep comes easy and I wake up the next morning refreshed and alone.

I don't see Lisa for three days.

59

*It's one year ago.

There's no note.

No voicemail. No text. Nothing. She's gone.

I could feel it when I came home. I double-check to make sure. Her closet is empty. Her shoes are gone. The place doesn't even smell like her anymore.

One picture is missing from the mantle.

Why would she take that one? It's a picture of us. Not a honeymoon shot. Nothing special. Just a candid shot someone took of us dancing at a friend's wedding. I always liked the picture and insisted it was the most romantic one we ever took. She hated the way she looked in it.

Why would she take that?

60

The pain in my side is killing me.

It's dull and sharp. Both. And it won't stop. So bad it wakes me up. Can't Cordoba give me something for this? Shouldn't I have a morphine drip or something?

Wait, why do I have a pain in my side?

I drift in and out of consciousness for a minute or an hour or a day until I can finally stay awake long enough to move my creaky arms. Each is stuffed with broken glass and I know my melted rubber face contorts with every rusty muscle fiber that gets put into service. I move my left hand far enough to run it over my side where I ache.

Stitches.

Feels like about eight inches of tidy sutures running along my side. Diagonal. Just above my hip. Those were not there when I went under. I'm still groggy from the anesthetic. Not thinking clearly. Did something happen? Was there an emergency that she had to perform surgery to correct? What could she have been doing down there? What organs are in that area? Not my heart. Not my lungs. Not my liver.

Where am I? Am I in a hospital? This is some kind of recovery room but not like I've been in before. Wasn't I just in Cordoba's living room? Did she have to call 911? Fuck, what if they figured out I was the guy who keeps trying to kill himself and I was transferred to a psych ward? That screws everything up.

Why would a psych ward be doing surgery on my lower back? And where is Cordoba, anyway?

But this can't be a hospital. The room is too big. It smells antiseptic but doesn't smell like death is around the corner. Definitely not a hospital.

This must still be Cordoba's place. Okay. I'm in a different room.

The fog of anesthesia is clearing and I remember being put under.

I did it.

I beat the fucking reaper. I had myself systematically killed and brought back to life in what I'm choosing to believe is a replicable procedure. I am Frankenstein with a victory laurel. Formerly a bag of bones and organs and muscle tissue bereft of life force until the good doctor shot me up with god knows how many volts and I came back to life. Dead. Then alive.

And that kiss. What was that? Right before I died she leaned in and kissed me. With her tongue. There's so much to process.

The stitches.

Why the fuck are there stitches in my side?

Cordoba walks in and checks the monitors without so much as a hello. Detachment, they call it in medical school. I wonder if she has a borderline personality. She must. Who else could do this work with such cold efficiency? I can appreciate her intellectual curiosity and unbridled ambition, but when it's not coupled with empathy what does that make her?

—What happened?

My voice sounds like I gargled sand.

—You tell me. Were you successful?

Oh, right.

It takes a second for the newly recovered memory to flash behind my eyes. I need to get this down soon. I'm trying to ignore the kiss and her detachment and what must be her raging case of crazytown to avoid losing what I came back with. There's only so much room in my head.

—Yeah.

—Good.

—What happened after that?

Why are there enough stitches to indicate a major unauthorized procedure happened while I was under? Surger-rape.

—You paid me.

What is she talking about? Would it be so hard to answer a question with a straightforward statement? Now we've got to play this game? She knows what I'm asking. I need to sketch. I need to get this down. I don't have time for this shit.

I paid her. What could that mean? You cut into my backside looking for my wallet? I paid you by letting you poke around my innards to satisfy some bizarre curiosity you have about—

Oh.

I know why the stitches are there. She wasn't fixing me. She was taking something out. Something someone badly needed and was willing to pay a lot of money for. Something I could spare. She's the middleman. I am a commodity.

I know what she means but I need her to say it.

—How did I pay you?

—Your kidney.

—You took it.

—I sold it. I told you I don't work for free. You've got another one.

That's a hell of a way to negotiate. How can I argue now? That organ is probably already pumping piss out of some diabetic in Russia by now. Besides, it's not like she's going to get it back for me. And I do have another one. I should be outraged. Indignant. Furious. But none of those will get me any closer to my goals and at best will result in an insincere apology. Better to be practical. Better to move forward.

—What if I want to do this again?

—You're covered. Kidney goes a long way these days.

Ah. I rub my hand over my stitches. Well, why not? I didn't have any big plans for my kidney. And now I'm playing with the bank's money. Enjoy the piss, Ivan.

—How long have I been out?

—A week. I kept you sedated and pumped you with some stuff I made to speed the recovery process.

Some stuff she made.

—So, did you find what you were looking for?

I want to ask her about the kiss but I force myself to focus on what's really important here. Maybe after I sketch. The mother-father-wallet-screaming-crying memory is chiseled into the wall of my mind but I know it won't last. I have to preserve it immediately. She seems genuinely interested but if I'm explaining anything to anyone it's to myself. I'm not wasting a second on anything that doesn't help preserve this precious mental cargo. Fuck the kiss.

—I have to draw something.

All I want to do is sleep, but every moment that passes means my memory fades farther back toward wherever it once was. She pauses long enough for me to realize that she thinks I should be sleeping, not drawing. But she must know I'm not going to close my eyes again until I sketch because she indicates a pad and pencils next to the bed.

—Thanks.

She cranks the bed up to a sitting position as I pull the pad onto my lap and start working. Moving my hands is exhausting and the muscle control involved in creating accurate drawings is intense but I'm afraid I've already lost plenty to the week of recovery. The images I get down are crude and childish in comparison to my earlier work, but they'll have to do. I decide to substitute words and arrows for details I can't capture perfectly. I spend the rest of the day sketching, stopping only when I can remember no other angles or nuances. By nightfall there are thirty-four new drawings.

Cordoba walks in and places a syringe and a glass vial of what I presume is magic recovery meds on the tray next to me.

—You go home tomorrow morning.

I have nothing else. I'm not going to a job. I have no wife. I am alone. This is now my life's work. The magic meds are my new best friends. My booster club. My pit crew. And Cordoba's creepy lab is my castle. Frankenstein's lair.

—How soon can I do it again?

—Three days.

The next time I wake up, Cordoba is gone.

I call out loudly several times but there's no response. And no note. Just the syringe and a vial of magic recovery meds she left on the tray, now rubber banded together. Hint, hint: Get the fuck out, Kidney Boy.

I feel better than when I came in, in spite of losing a major organ. I'm aching and crusty, but there's a fire burning inside me now. My body feels ninety-five and my mind feels twenty-six. A sweet hum in the back of my head tells me this is going to work out. I think this might be what hope feels like.

I dress as fast as I can, which in reality is quite slow. God, dying hurts. The wound where my kidney used to be is still sensitive. I feel it with every move I make. On the other hand, it's been a week already so how much of that is psychosomatic? Probably a lot. I'd love some meds to put that pain to sleep but I'm betting the recovery serum I'm headed home to inject will cover that.

I can't get that kiss out of my mind. I wish that I could, as it serves no purpose aside from confounding me. Was that some sort of goodbye thing in case I didn't make it? She's never expressed an emotion in my presence before and she barely knows me.

Plus she was masturbating. Hmm.

I find Cordoba intimidating. Impotence-inducing intimidating and, even if I could get it up, I've got more important things to deal with than a one-night stand with a mad scientist. And that's not to mention how fucking weird it is that she chose the moment I was dying to lay that on me. I suspect she thought I was out. Maybe I was. Maybe I made the whole thing up. A heroin induced delusion. I know that's not true and it makes her creepier than ever.

I can see through an open door there's a hallway to somewhere. The rest of the loft that I'll never see. The other half of her life. I guess part of me is still human because it's tempting to take a quick look around before I head out. Open her drawers, riffle through her mail, check her browser history. Get a deeper understanding of who she is. Is there a family? A boyfriend? A girlfriend? Pictures? I can't see her having any of them, but that doesn't mean it's not true. From an anthropological standpoint, a little look-see through Cordoba's personal effects couldn't be anything but fascinating.

Last time I snooped through someone's stuff, I found a stack of unopened letters from my father. Had to be a hundred of them jammed into the back of Foster Mother's closet. Not sure what her plan was. To give them to me when I was an adult and it was too late to have a relationship with the man? To wait until he quit sending them and then burn the lot en masse? To save me the pain of a bi-weekly reminder that my father killed my mother and was staring at the walls in a concrete box instead of teaching me how to use a stick shift? She probably didn't think it out beyond getting them out of everyone's sight as soon as possible. She was always a coward.

I had convinced myself that he hated me and stopped writing after his initial barrage. For the first week I got letters from him every day. They were always waiting for me on the kitchen table when I got home. Foster Father sniggered and shook his head to make sure I knew he thought my father was a loser. But I loved getting them. Loved them so much I ripped the envelopes open right in front of Foster Father and savored every word. Reading them was the only time I could hear my father's voice in my head. I was scared and confused and this was the safest interaction I could have with him. A one-way conversation that I could replay as often as I liked.

Not that I would have written him back. Or maybe I would have eventually. When I found the stack in the closet I read one of the letters at random but that was all I could handle. It didn't really matter anyway. He had died three months earlier.

Cordoba's open door stares back at me. The hallway leads to a bedroom. It must be a bedroom because I think I see the corner of a comforter. There has to be a closet back there somewhere. I'm sitting in her secret illegal operating room that's practically out in the open. Whatever is stuffed in the back of her closet must be exponentially worse. I'm not going to look.

I roll up my drawings carefully, grab the meds, and leave. The sooner I recover, the sooner I can die again.

*It's ten months ago.

I walk through the office trying to avoid eye contact with anyone who might say something to me or, worse, ask me a question.

I'm at my desk. I have seventeen voicemails and sixty-five unopened e-mails. What the hell could be so urgent? I'm an estate attorney for Christ's sake.

The e-mails are the usual bullshit about meetings and marginally important questions that would be so much clearer if the asker had gotten off their fat ass and walked down the hall to ask them in person. As I scroll down they get more and more shrill. Where's the Holman file I promised? Why wasn't I in the staff meeting? Why am I not answering my phone? Where am I?

Babies.

On top of all that it looks like the date and time on my computer are off. About a day ahead.

I check my phone to reset them correctly. It says the same thing.

Today is Wednesday.

I thought it was Tuesday.

I would have sworn it was Tuesday.

What happened to Tuesday?

I'm wearing the same suit I wore Monday. I stink. I haven't shaved.

This is my first sober blackout, at least to the best of my knowledge. Maybe there have been others but I don't remember. That's the point, right? I stand in front of my humming desktop machine trying to understand what happened. Trying to remember. Last thing I can recall is leaving the office Monday evening. Nothing special. It was a fairly grueling day as usual, but mostly because I now find my work a contrivance of this modern age that's defined by the finicky and petty. I left Monday night. Hailed a cab. Black.

It's a clean black. A seamless transition between thirty-six hours ago and one minute ago. As if a surgeon came by and nipped the intervening time out. Gone.

I check my phone to see if there are any outgoing calls that might jog my memory. Nothing. Plenty of incoming messages, all from the office. None marked as listened to.

I left Monday night. Hailed a cab. Black.

I shut everything down and leave.

Two hours later I'm standing outside an apartment building on the Upper East Side.

It was a bad idea to come here like this. I'm drunker than I would like to be and I have no plan beyond asking her to come back. Maybe I'll beg.

I ring the buzzer and wait.

If you bothered to track down the bartender with the wonky eye and the gray teeth at that Lower East Side bar I can't remember the name of, you could ask him about the night I told him about the girl who was going to have my children.

Obviously, it was Lisa, and I doubt the bartender would remember me slurring my prediction through the haze of my umpteenth martini as I watched her score an eight ball for us from her dealer who delivered, but I did it and he heard it and if she and I had stayed together longer I would have been one hundred percent correct. And then she would have never left. Not if we had a kid. Lisa was like that.

I knew. This was a few years ago. We weren't even dating at the time and I knew. Maybe I'll tell her the bartender story and see how that goes. I think I might have told her that one before.

A younger couple comes out the front door. They're in the middle of a fight and so wrapped up in themselves they wouldn't notice if I darted in behind them before the door shuts.

No.

That would be bad form.

She'll let me in or she won't.

An hour later I stop ringing her buzzer and go home. It was a dumb plan.

63

(Dear me.)

It would appear that the absurd little schemes of our man are beginning to pay dividends. Just look at the old boy trudge down the street. Such determination! Such focus! A fugue state of ataxic self-importance. A midden of ego. It's a far cry from the preening jackass he presented himself as only weeks ago.

Our man can barely maintain an upright posture, for heaven's sake! He is weaving. Careening even. And yet, there is the unavoidable impression that he is unstoppable. Indomitable!

Let's review his most recent history. Two productive excursions across the transom of the afterlife to collect bounty of immeasurable personal value followed each time by an immediate return trip to his barracoon of living and breathing with the rest of humanity. The pressing question on our collective minds is exactly how long he can continue this grueling cycle. The human body can withstand only so much abuse and there can be little doubt that the old boy is pushing his physical being to its design limits. It is unnatural. Untenable. Surely, the awl of God's pride will be making its point known in the near future. What a foolish little man.

But save yourself the trouble of cautioning him. He is resolved to move forward regardless of the price tag. Intentionally blind to obvious caveats. Purposefully deaf to well-meaning advice. Willfully ignorant in the face of common sense.

And on he marches. Head down. Chuffing audibly from the effort.

Pay close attention to the pride of gentlemen walking past our man at this very moment. There are three in total. The alpha male of the group allows himself a double take and his face clouds as he can't help but think to himself that he recognizes 'that bum' from somewhere. He slows and watches with knitted eyebrows and furrowed forehead as the old boy toddles past. But no, he says to himself, the chap I'm thinking of was of a most robust demeanor. Strapping. Not shriveled and stooped and hobbled. Not reeking of last week's gin and this week's body odor. No, no that couldn't be Christian Franco. Perhaps a distant relative or simply a random stranger who bears striking resemblance. A distressed doppelganger. Imagine the chances! Oh, the fellows back at the office will have a hearty laugh at this encounter.

He says nothing and moves on, but only a few steps later, unable to shake the conviction, he turns again to have a closer look. Based on the erratic behavior of the hobo in question, the intrepid gentleman is well aware that he is putting himself at great risk of receiving a scurrilous tongue lashing, if not a homemade knife to the gut, but proceeds with his impromptu plan nevertheless.

Our man's name is called out but to no avail. And again, only louder and with a degree of petulance. The gentleman has begun to feel the thrill of challenge dripping down the back of his neck. What began as simple curiosity has become a game he is unwilling to lose.

Christian! he calls out, but the old boy continues his grunting trundle away from our new friend.

Christian Franco! he calls out to this lower-caste occupant who appears to be ignoring his advances. Oh, the cheeky gumption of petty men. How often does a nonaction become misconstrued as a challenge? A silence interpreted as a threat? Nothing as something? It is no more than flapdoodle and malarkey, but this is the nature of adult males.

The gentleman's compatriots have returned to him, after noticing their leader missing from the pack. He explains the conundrum he finds himself in.

That's Christian Franco and the gentleman intends to prove it to them.

64

I decide the only thing I can spend my remaining cash on is food.

Which means I can't afford to pay for a cab and I can't take the ride and beat the fare because I can barely walk much less outrun some fat Czech driver. Looks like I'm shuffling home.

It's late afternoon. There are no windows in Cordoba's lab so this comes as a surprise to me. Could have been midnight for all I knew. I head up Allen and make a left on Broome when I hear my name. They must have been calling me for a while because by the time it registers whoever is calling sounds agitated.

It's a man. He may be someone I recognize.

—Franco?! Christian?!

It's a guy from the law firm. I think his name is DiRienz. Frank. Or James. We used to be office friends. Sometimes we got drunk together. I sort of remember him. He talks very loud. As I recall, he felt it made him a better litigator. It didn't. He smiles and I can't tell if he's happy to see me or happy to see that I look like a deranged homeless guy.

—Dude, what the fuck?

He must have walked by me and realized who I am a few steps later. He's walking back up toward me followed by a gaggle of adoring douchebags from the office. I used to know some of them.

—I heard you got fired for driving a car into a bank or some shit.

I find them hostile although I doubt they intend to be. They're smiling with their perfect teeth. Leering interchangeable hyenas. I can see they're shocked by my appearance. I should be embarrassed but I'm enjoying their discomfort on so many levels.

—Aren't you supposed to be in rehab or something?

That's not concern in his voice. I'm silent because I have nothing to say to Frank or James DiRienz. He's not concerned for me. He's digging for a good story to tell the boys at the Monday morning staff meeting. His eyes are eating me up.

—Well, um, it's great to see you. Are you working or . . .

He trails off when even he realizes what an idiotic question it is. Yes, FrankOrJames. I'm working. I'm running M&A at Goldman. I'm heading up NASA's next Mars expedition. I just signed a three-picture deal with Warner Bros.

Look at me. I'll never work again. It's not an unsettling thought.

I turn to walk off and as I do, I bump into a guy in a chicken costume handing out flyers for a local restaurant. The impact knocks my arm and sends my syringe/magic meds pack flying out of my pocket to the ground. The ground! FrankOrJames and his dipshit buddies all see it. And there they've got their story for Monday. Not only do they see the syringe fall out but they watch me scramble to grab it. It's my lifeblood and I act like it. The street is crowded and if someone steps on it, I'm fucked.

I drop to all fours and lunge for the vial before an old lady crushes it with her chunky, sensible shoes. I'm flat on my stomach across the sidewalk. Who cares. I hold my meds and syringe close to my chest and stand back up. FrankOrJames and company eye me very closely. What am I supposed to do here, boys? Take a bow? Fuck off.

I start to move past them when FrankOrJames puts a hand on my shoulder. I'm not sure why he feels the gesture is appropriate. I don't think we were that close. We might have done some blow in a bathroom once. Maybe I'm wrong. I know when he walks away the first thing he'll do is wash his hands.

—Bro, are you okay? You need to talk to someone?

Mmm-hmm. Why don't you give Arnold Rosen a call for me? Oh, never mind, I already solved this problem myself. I cracked the code. Something you, FrankOrJames, will never do. But I don't feel like explaining that to you because I guaran-fucking-tee you wouldn't understand. Take your little news update back to the hive and choke on it, bro.

—I have to go.

I move past the slack-jawed meatheads with their padded bellies and continue toward my home. I wonder if they're taking pictures of me with their phones but I don't care enough to look back over my shoulder. This little incident shouldn't take too long to get back to Harry. That doesn't bother me. I'm done with him.

My legs start to warm up as I shamble along. Soon it almost feels like a walk. Like I'm human.

I don't hear the footsteps of whoever is following me. I feel them. It strikes me as absurd that DiRienz would continue the ruse of concerned former coworker this far. He was never that committed to the joke as I recall. More of a one-liner kind of guy. But I know he's there and it's one more thing I have to deal with. I can't have anyone interfering with what I'm doing no matter how much they think they can help me.

I turn up Bowery. This will do the trick. DiRienz was most likely headed for happy hour and every step he takes after me puts him that much farther away from his next Jägerbomb. Yet I still feel him. Good god, could it be that he has an iota of altruistic tendencies in his dinky little brain? Impossible. So why is he still there?

Every ounce of energy I have left I consider sacred, but I decide to invest some of it in turning around to tell Frank or James to fuck right off. Pretty sure it will pay off in the long run.

He's not there.

My side of the street is empty. On the other side an old lady pushes a cart the opposite direction. So what was all that about?

Side effects. I'm still waking up. I was dead only days before this and in a coma until thirty-six hours ago. There must be lingering effects. How could there not be?

I start moving again and right away I know I'm not alone.

I can't hear the footsteps. But I know someone is there. Was there a doorway or something to hide in that I missed? Where are they?

I turn left on Kenmare and speed my pace up as much as I can, which isn't much. Halfway down the block I turn back. There's a shopkeeper pulling a hose out to spray down his sidewalk. And a woman paying for parking. And a guy walking my way. Casually walking toward me with long confident strides. Smirking.

I'm projecting way too much on this guy. He's no one. I cross the street anyway. Fuck it. I'll go over here and watch him pass.

The syringe and meds are still in my front pocket in the vice grip of my hand. I am taking no chances.

On the other side of the street I look back to see the guy with the smirk has followed me over here. Or he had business over here and came over without thinking twice about me. It's possible. Calm down.

No way this guy is from the city. Who smirks? And what's with the mustache? He's got a major Goose Gossage mustache. Maybe he's on his way to shoot some porn.

I turn and move my feet as quickly as they'll go. I know Goose McSmirk is still behind me because he's whistling. Who whistles? That fucking mustache makes me crazy. I'm hyper-focusing because of stress. It's a release. It must be.

I turn up Elizabeth and I know I'm about a block and a half from my house. Five seconds later I look back and see him make the same turn. He's gaining quickly but I've only seen him walking casually. Is he running when I'm not looking? He looks like he's in shape, but I don't think college sprinters can make that kind of time. How is he moving so fast? He's not making eye contact, but he is looking past me every time I look back. Like he's looking ahead to where I'm going. My heart is working hard now, although I can't be sure how much is anxiety and how much is basic necessity to keep my worn-out body upright and moving forward. That whistling. I hate tourists. They're always such happy simpletons. He must be from out of town. With that corny, dated outfit.

I'm worried about tripping and landing on my medicine. That has to remain my top priority. Get the meds home in one piece and shoot them into my god damn arm. There can be nothing else. Keep moving.

I tell myself he's not moving faster but I know he is. He's gaining. I won't look back. I don't have to. The whistling is louder. Can I run? Is that possible? Is it smart? What if he is following me? Why? What could he possibly want from me? I don't know this guy. I have nothing. Does he want my meds? That's not happening. But do I want him to know where I live? I should circle the block and see if he follows but I know I don't have the energy for that. I'm heading straight for my apartment. At this rate, we'll reach my front door at the same time.

I'm sweating and it's awkward to speed stagger with my hand in my pocket. I slide the meds out and use both hands to hold them. My mind is strong. I'll will myself to move my legs faster. I am the Lance Armstrong of Frankensteins. If I need to run I'll run. My legs move and I'm gaining speed.

Don't fall don't fall don't fall don't fall don't fall don't fall don't fall don't fall.

I can't bring myself to turn around to see if he's speeded up as well. He might still be whistling, but running without crashing is taking every ounce of focus I have so I don't know for sure. I'm moving better than I expected. The body is an incredible thing. I turn left on Prince and I'm half a block away from my building.

As I approach the front door I realize I don't have the coordination to pull out my key with my one free hand while I'm going this fast. I don't even know if I still have my key. I stopped locking the door to my apartment months ago. Sometimes I left it wide open when I went out. But the front door of the building is always locked. I don't have the time to fumble around and I can't do anything without putting my meds somewhere first. Fuck, am I going to have to confront this guy right now?

My neighbor walks out. I race past her before the door can close and indicate back toward Goose.

—Don't let that guy in here.

I slam the front door in my neighbor's confused/irritated face and head up the stairs as fast as my pathetic quads will let me.

Down the hall and into my apartment. Meds on the table by the entry. Slam the door. Lock all three locks. Turn my back to the door and slide down to the floor.

My meds are safe. I'm locked in.

Fuck that guy.

I'm sweating bullets and feel like crying.

I breathe deep. It feels good.

My heart begins to slow back down to normal.

BOOMBOOMBOOMBOOMBOOMBOOMBOOMBOOM!

Someone pounds on my door and I don't have to check the peephole to know who it is. I jump away and watch the sliver of a shadow underneath. Two confident feet face the door.

BOOMBOOMBOOMBOOMBOOMBOOMBOOMBOOM!

I don't move a muscle or say a fucking word and neither does he for two full minutes.

And then he leaves. I hear him strut down the stairs and I'm alone.

65

I'm at FedEx Office.

No one gives me a second look because homeless and crazy people come in here every day to kill time, warm up, and organize their tatty bag of newspaper clippings and scribbled, illegible rants. By comparison, I'm a slight improvement.

I waited around my apartment for a while, eager to shoot up but reluctant to relinquish control with that weirdo lurking. And then I started looking at my drawings. Two hours later, I realized I had been so deeply focused on my art that I've forgotten about my creepy shadow from this afternoon. If he was even real. We never made any physical contact and, technically, I never saw him outside my door. I assumed he was there. There's so much missing in my collection of memories. I've got to fill in some blanks and it didn't take much to convince myself that I had been hallucinating the smirking mustache man. Goose. How absurd. There's no one following me. I'm exhausted and my mind is playing horrible tricks on me. The knocking was probably the building super or a neighbor. That could be true. I tell myself it is. I have important things to do.

I know I have to get answers, and now I've got a willing accomplice to kill me as often as I'd like. The formula is there. But, honestly, how long can that go on? The toll is immense and I'm deteriorating quickly. I need to focus, to target specific memories. I need help.

I need Ella.

What I would have spent on food tonight, I'm spending on copies. My gamble is that my meds will make up the difference. Or I'll steal a steak. But if I can create a catalyst to enhance my efforts, it's worth skipping dinner.

I know Ella remembers something and even if it's only a minor detail that might save me a trip to the afterlife or at least offer some landmarks to look for while I'm there. I need to jar her memory. I know she has scar tissue in there. I want to know what it is. That's my scar tissue too.

Ella has one of the loudest voices I've ever heard. For the most part she's soft spoken and reasonable. She's nice. Until she's not nice. And then she yells.

I'm making copies of all my back-from-the-dead drawings to show Ella. Let her yell at me. That seems to be when we communicate best. And lately, that's the only time she can be honest with me.

I'm at Ella's by nine.

The house is dark and I know before I get to the front door that no one's home. I should have called but she would have only hung up on me if she had even picked up the phone. This was my only choice and it didn't pay off.

The doors and windows are locked and I don't want to break in. She's pissed enough already. Also it wouldn't do me any good. I need to interact with her.

My options are limited. Abandon this plan, go home, and shoot up. I'll be back in action in a few days and I can continue my harvesting scheme. Or I can wait here until she gets home from wherever she is and try to talk her into spending some quality time with me.

Or I could leave the drawings.

I hop up and start stuffing the sketches through the mail slot. She'll know where they came from. She'll know they're for her. She'll have to do some explaining to her kids and her husband but she'll get through that.

I wonder how much she's told Tim. Not much I bet. I bet she changes the subject or straight-up lies when he asks about her childhood. Although, he's so god damn self-centered he probably never asks. Which is why she was attracted to him in the first place. His egotism was the safest place for Ella to hide. The soothing comfort of someone else's bloated self-worth. Poor thing.

I give up trying to land each drawing on top of the last. They're going everywhere. Drifting left and right all over the foyer floor. She's going to come home to a bona fide mess. Maybe that's a good thing. I'm a mess. This is me on the floor, Ella. I'm lying here asking you to look at me. Look at me with the innocent eyes of the three-year-old you were and tell me what you see. Strip away the tired cynicism and defeated hopelessness from your worldview and look at me. Tell me what connects. I know something here touches you deep down. You were there.

I'm fading. The adrenaline that accompanied my realization that help might only be a shocking drawing away has played itself out and I'm running on fumes. I finish feeding the last few drawings through the mail slot and walk away.

Look at me, Ella.

I creep back to my building, watchful and wary of my friend with the smirk. Maybe I hadn't so thoroughly convinced myself he was an illusion after all. I tell myself it's ludicrous and then I decide to play it safe anyway. I know that this might be the dawn of paranoia but my fear feels so authentic I can't help but indulge it. I see nothing suspicious as I turn onto my block. No one following me. No one waiting. Nothing unusual. I have my key out early anyway.

If you think you're crazy, you're not. That's the rule, isn't it?

I stole two plastic-wrapped bagels with cream cheese from a deli on the way back and my stomach is eating itself in anticipation. My overwhelming anxiety won't let me take them out of my pocket. As if the Korean I stole them from is waiting in a shadow to pounce once he confirms I walked out with something. I make myself wait. It's ridiculous but I do it anyway.

My apartment smells like home and I rip into a bagel the second I get the door locked. It's the most delicious thing I've ever eaten.

The next thing I know it's dawn. I've spent the last nine hours hanging and rearranging my drawings on the exposed brick in my living room. I had a thought that they would be easier to digest if I could look at them as one piece. The sum of the parts must mean more than the individuals. It took me this long to get them right. Eleven rows. I'm not sure how many columns. My eyes are blurring.

Stepping back I can take in the whole crop I have harvested as one unintelligible story. The world's worst graphic novel. Why these images? Of the entire catalogue I had to choose from, why these? They have nothing to do with each other and have zero discernible relation to my life now.

What's still in my head? I could fill Giants stadium. For now I have this awful comic strip of a life on my lonely, lonely wall.

I know there's something here. Just as I know there's plenty missing.

There's nothing more I can do with this and I know that if I go any further, I'll collapse.

Time for the needle.

I'm late for it and I know Cordoba will be expecting me sooner than I'm going to show up but that's the way it's going to have to be. I'm already paid up. She can wait.

I fill up a gallon bottle of water and set it next to where I intend to put myself out. My mouth waters at the thought of what's about to happen.

I tie off.

I shoot up.

I pass out.

Black.

The next forty-eight hours are a blur of the deepest, darkest sleep I've ever experienced, nonsensical rambling, crying jags, fist pounding, howling, and sweating. As far as I can remember, anyway.

I wake up once again soaked in urine, shit, and vomit. There's some blood also, but I couldn't tell you what orifice it came out of. The water bottle is long empty. I'm across the room from where I started.

But I feel better. Not strong. Not bulletproof. But better. Revitalized.

I fill the water bottle up and drink the entire thing immediately. I wonder what day it is and then remember it no longer matters. The water hits my system and wakes me up further. Whatever was in those syringes is a bloody miracle.

I shuffle into the bathroom to take the first shower I've had in I don't know how many days (weeks?) and see myself in the mirror. Such lines in my face. Not just wrinkles, but deep crags. My stitched up kidney wound is nothing but a red line that no longer hurts.

I'm raring to kill myself again and I know Cordoba must be waiting but I stay under the shower to clean the last few days off my body. Scrub away the despair. Soak in some lukewarm hope.

*It's nine months ago.

I'm standing outside the apartment building I'm almost positive Lisa is staying in.

The lights are on in the third floor unit that might belong to her friend from college. From what I've gathered the few times she's spoken to me, Lisa is dating a man I don't know. Not sure if it's the same guy who almost got her pregnant last year or if it's a new guy.

I'm staring at the windows and remembering a discussion I had with her about the Beach Boys' song 'Good Vibrations.' She had pointed out that taken at face value it's a beautiful song about a boy in love with a girl and the magical bond they share. But listen a little closer, give the lyrical intent some leeway, and you've got a true stalker situation involving a guy who is picking up 'vibrations' from a girl he sees but possibly has never met. Doesn't sound like this girl is aware of the vibes she's putting out but the guy feels like they're oh-so-tangible and give him the okay to not only fall in love with her but to construct a mythical relationship and consequently approach her with the good news.

Think about that little chat. I can't see it lasting long and if it did there would be police and restraining orders and judges and god knows what else.

What I've learned from Lisa regarding her love life is thin and largely conjecture, as the only time I can get her to open up at all is by picking a fight over something small when I trick her into answering the phone. The new guy is in real estate. A developer, so you know he's a dick.

194

Two weeks ago she was in my (our) apartment when I came home. She still has a key, but I never lock the door anymore. The conversation was short.

—I want a divorce.

What am I going to do? Fight? I can only imagine the mustering that went on before she came over to confront me. Working herself up. Practicing in front of the mirror. Promising the developer she would go through with it. Getting a pep talk from Fucking Michelle. Her jaw was set and she was rehearsed.

—Christian, I want a divorce.

She made it a point to look at me when she said it but once the hard part was done she found other things to focus on. Bracing (hoping) for a fight, I suspect. But I wouldn't do it. Not that night, at least. She had indicated to me she wanted out in so many ways over the months previous that saying the words out loud were a simple matter of convention.

I wonder if men and women look at divorce the same way they do marriage. I thought of it as an ending. A finale. I think she might have seen it as an invitation to a deeper dialogue. But I knew that wasn't going to happen that night. This was part of the grieving process. It could take months. So, I gave her what she needed.

— . . . Okay.

And here I am. I don't really have a plan besides watching what may or may not be the apartment she's living in these days. I suppose I'm hoping she'll walk out and we'll see each other and I'll say something meaningful. I don't know what that will be but perhaps being near her will inspire something breathtaking or coherent. Hopefully, I'll get some vibrations.

I'm not stalking Lisa. I was her husband.

67

Cordoba isn't surprised when I show up.

She says nothing about me being (according to the newspapers on the way over) a full day and a half late. Nothing seems to shake her. I guess that's one of the benefits of having a borderline personality. I wonder what she would react to. Zombies? Aliens? Probably not.

She's prepped and ready as if she knew I would arrive at this exact moment. I sit on the edge of the operating table and she's strictly business. Asks about how I'm feeling. Checks my vitals. Tests my pupils. Takes a lot of notes. The file she's keeping on me is much thicker than last time. She must have been doing some data analyzation since I left. So dedicated. Can she get published for this kind of work? Who would believe it? She'd more likely get thrown in jail. The notes can only be for her. Or for when she dies. A brilliant manifesto published posthumously and forever heralding her as the great one who solved mankind's problems. Like Timothy McVeigh.

She preps my injection points, working quickly and efficiently as if I weren't even there. I am a lab rat. I am living data. I am a collection of impersonal test results.

Did I hallucinate the kiss last time? I'm doubting everything now.

Cordoba leans me back and straps me in. Both wrists. Both ankles. My chest. I'm shirtless and covered with monitor pads connected to beeping machines. I am a dissected frog valued solely for research purposes.

It's go time.

She looks over her tray of syringes arranged neatly in a row and selects the one closest to us.

—Are you ready to die again?

I'm so ready. And I'm terrified. I am confident. And I am a little boy who wants to run. I'm scared. And I'm happy. I'm strapped down. I am in control.

—Do it.

She slips the first needle in and glides the plunger in. Instantly I relax. Her eyes light up a little as she watches it hit me. God damn, heroin feels good. This is the greatest invention ever. I'm so happy and my head rolls around but she won't break eye contact with me.

Wait.

This isn't the same feeling I had last time. What the fuck?

—This . . . is . . . different.

—We're trying something new.

Something new. Like what? Steroids? Angel Juice? I want to have a conversation about this change in the agreed-upon plan but even saying those last three words was a struggle. She tricked me again. She's going rogue and there isn't a thing I can do. I have willfully submitted myself to an unknown medical experiment with a lunatic doctor.

Cordoba inserts the second syringe. Even if I weren't lashed to the table, I could do nothing to stop her. Her hair falls over her face like Lisa's used to. Usually, she's got it pulled back in a tight ponytail. When did she let it down? The second plunger goes down.

Oh my god.

She's so into this she can barely speak. I hear or see or understand that the monitor readings are starting to slow. I'm drifting off. My eyelids are ten pound weights. I don't know why I'm fighting this but I am. Cordoba's hand is down her skirt. She's touching herself and staring into my eyes.

I didn't hallucinate the kiss.

My eyes drift down and I notice I'm sporting an immense hard-on. When did my pants come undone? How did I not notice her doing that?

Cordoba hikes her skirt and climbs on top of me. She slides me inside of her and moves her hips slowly back and forth as she takes her time with the third syringe.

The last plunger goes down and I get a rush of soft, warm goodness that swallows me up whole. As I fade out I hear my own monitors flat lining as Cordoba moans.

Jesus. She's a necrophiliac.

And I'm dead.

Black.

White.

The White.

I have become comfortable in these surroundings. Maybe that's a good thing. The White is bright and clean and perfect like I remember it. Sterile, sparkling white and yet soothing and comfortable. Like I'm a welcome guest. I'm supposed to be here.

My mind is now the entirety of my being. I am a thought process and nothing more. Flexible to turn at will without physical limitations. There is no up or down here. There is everything and nothing. I can move at the speed of light. What's faster than the speed of light? That's how fast I can move. But I don't move anywhere because this is where I need to be. This is what I need to be. I am The White.

Waiting for the whoosh.

Are we still fucking?

My entire existence is now devoted to harvesting my treasured, long-lost memories, and the sand in my Vaseline is this thought that while I'm dead, somewhere back in the world of gravity and clocks and parking tickets, Cordoba is having sex with my corpse.

The heroin felt different. If I'm crudely reverse engineering the formula she used, I'm guessing she added some Viagra (or its homemade equivalent) to the mix and timed everything so I'd be hard and dead simultaneously. I'm not sure why I care. That body is of little use to me now. This is where I want to live. Surrounded by the truth of my life. Enveloped by my own all-knowing subconscious. But the god damn questions about Cordoba are tainting the purity of The White this time. Why couldn't my kidney be enough?

A faint wisp of the whoosh hits me and I know the memory storm is coming. I'm ready. But I'm not focused. Why couldn't she just kill me and let me do my thing? Now I'm here in Perfectland, distracted when I should be concentrating on this rare opportunity.

How long have I been out? Is this death and rebirth experience a small sliver of time that only seems like it lasts longer or is it a much more extended period that I only remember a tiny bit from? It can't be too long. No matter how good of a doctor she is there are limitations to what the human body can do. I'm guessing time slows here in limbo. I'm not playing by the same rules she is. She's probably got no more than two minutes to work her magic. How long can that two minutes last in The White time?

The whoosh is growing. I try to let go of everything in my head. Clear it out to make room. I am empty. I am Zen. I am ready.

Can I ejaculate when I'm dead? I wonder if there was a little extra something in the mix to help out with that. That seems like a lot of effort to put into fucking a dead guy, but then how often does she get that opportunity? She does look a lot like Lisa.

I turn my presence toward the sound. Focus, you idiot. An infinitely wide and unimaginably tall wall of memories rushes toward me. The anticipation is delicious.

WHOOSH!

The memories race past fast enough to scorch me but they don't. They are a cool, calming breeze that feels so good against my tired soul that I want to close my eyes and let them wash over me. But I can't.

There I am at prom.

There I am mowing the lawn.

Arguing with a clerk about fixtures in the Home Depot lighting section.

Hitting the lobby button in an elevator.

Bench pressing.

Tapping the snooze button.

Negotiating my second big salary raise.

Standing in the foyer of my Brooklyn home.

I need that one.

I focus and will the memory toward me or myself toward it. I can't tell the difference and don't care. Faster and faster we move together until it hits me like a slap on the face that I deserve and I'm there.

I'm eight.

I'm home in Brooklyn in the house with the stoop. I'm in the doorway between the foyer and the hall that leads back to our kitchen. I know I'm scared, but I'm not sure why. Ella isn't in the room, but maybe she recently left or is coming back or hiding. I feel like she's near. My mother is pleading her case to a uniformed policeman standing just inside the closed front door. He's a tall, muscular guy, looking at her and faced away from me. He's got cop forearms. I can tell he's confident even from behind. In control of the situation. The opposite of my mother who looks like she's spinning out. She's twisting a lock of hair like she always used to when she was stressed. I had forgotten that until now.

I have to remember every detail. I have to drink this in. Soak up everything. Suck the marrow out of this memory.

My mother looks from the cop to me and back to the cop. She seems upset. Worried. Jumpy. I never thought of her as impatient, but maybe she was. Or maybe it's the situation.

—I don't know what else to do. Tony's not leaving me any choice.

She's almost whispering to the cop but I can hear every word. I'm not sure she cares. Her eyes are sad every time she looks at me and back to him. I don't know where my father is. She seems so desperate.

Remember this smell. Take in the smallest details. My mother's dress. The mail piled up next to the front door. Ella's toys in the hallway. The broken chain lock on the front door. The four-day-old bruise on my mother's eye.

The cop puts his hand on my mother's shoulder.

—I understand.

He pauses for a second, I suppose to instill confidence.

—Will he be home anytime soon?

My mother relaxes somewhat and shakes her head no.

I'm terrified and I don't know why. Where is Ella? I know she was just here.

The cop starts turning to look my way but the sound is already fading and I know I'll be out of here before he gets all the way around.

69

(Tsk, tsk.)

Tenacity is so admirable a quality one is tempted to overlook the circumstances that caused the good doctor to find herself in this situation where it is so valuable. She is putting forth a herculean effort, unyielding in her determination and so thoroughly stubborn as to be valiant, but only because she has allowed herself to be in a position in which nothing short of this strenuous exertion will extricate her from what is undeniably a situation problematic to explain away to even the dullest of authorities. She has made a misstep.

The old boy is dead and gone at her hands and she is, understandably, becoming increasingly frustrated with regards to what are beginning to look like fruitless attempts at revival.

Christian should be back by now.

Perhaps she was a little too long enjoying the fruits of her labor. Orgasmic to the point of distraction. Greedy. Sloppy. This is the dilemma of her unique flavor of arousal. The sole form of sexual activity that is satisfying to her presents itself so rarely that when she has the opportunity to indulge herself, it is no small matter to stop. She was an animal. Her hair is tousled. Her lower back moist from perspiration. Her brain addled with endorphins. For a brief moment, she was sated. But now there is this to contend with.

The dead man who has trusted her with what is left of his life waits patiently for the good doctor to ply her oh-so-specialized trade on him. This is the sole purpose for which he sought her out. Suicide he can accomplish on his own time. Reanimation was the promise she made and has yet to fulfill, this round anyway. The old boy will never know, of course. He is expired, and should he remain so, well, there would be no way to inform him of the doctor's failure, and also no need. If an afterlife exists, he will come to understand that there is only one way he could have arrived there. Should he be revived, Cordoba will likely tell him the procedure went swimmingly. Precisely as planned. And he will be none the wiser. But as a matter of pride, the good doctor is resolved to remedy the situation. This is her job.

She pounds on our man's chest.

Pumps fluids into his veins.

Talks forcefully to him.

Nothing yet.

But then, he has always been difficult.

To say she is nervous would be inaccurate. Anxious, perhaps. But only because she is acutely aware of the steep plummet in the likelihood of success as time marches mercilessly forward. Eight minutes of death preceding revival is not unheard of in some operating theaters, but you would only know that number because of the successful efforts of a team of world-class medical professionals working in concert to bring the recently deceased back to life. Cordoba is alone to administer her homemade remedies and chest compressions. It is draining, grinding her will more with each passing second. But as I have mentioned, she is tenacious.

70

Black.

I know I'm alive because I was dreaming.

It was a dream I've had before about Lisa and seeing her one last time. Seeing her happy, that is. I can only remember the bad times when I'm awake. Wallow in them. The good times are locked away somewhere, like my childhood. The difference being I made the conscious choice to hide the happy times with Lisa in a deep, dark corner of my mind. Not as punishment. To save me from further breakdown. Remembering what I lost when she left can only hurt so I don't deal with it.

This must be a pattern I set up so long ago. Something in my head decided when things get bad enough, you simply put any and all records of them in a nice tight package and store that away for later. Not too shabby for an eight-year-old. As a thirty-eight year-old, though, I should probably rethink the logic. What would the harm be in wallowing a bit every once in a while? I guess that's what my dreams are trying to tell me. A mental movie trailer for what could be seen if I would man up and go through what people have told me is a healthy, if arduous, process.

Whenever I have this dream, at least eight times in the last year and a half, I recognize it immediately. As soon as it starts. It feels good. It's not that I know exactly what's going to happen next, but I do go through a bit of a calming déjà vu. I know what is coming will be good. Like I've come home to a place I had forgotten about but know very well. Later that day, when I'm fully awake, I forget that I had the dream. Or

I repress it once again. Whatever I do, there's no acknowledgment on any conscious level that it was there. I suppose whatever purpose the dream served will have been accomplished. An option presented. An itch scratched. My mind will put it back on the shelf until the next time it is needed.

The dream is simple. Lisa and I lie in bed together, wrapped around each other. Laughing. I don't know what we thought was so funny. Doesn't matter. It feels good. Her skin against mine. The smell of her hair. Her unguarded giggle. At some point she gets up and walks out of the room and I don't mind. I know she's coming right back but I always wake up before she does. Tell me again why this is a bad thing, Christian. Tell me why you won't let yourself remember the good times. Surely, the pain of acceptance can't outweigh the value of fond memories?

I am a petulant child. My mind is a living, breathing tantrum. I am screaming NO at myself. The memories are there, but I don't deserve them.

She's just left the room and I'm lying there thinking I have to tell her something when she comes back but, as always, she doesn't make it.

The dream fades fast, and just as fast reality creeps in to replace it in my half-awake mind. Lisa's presence is shunted away in favor of the feel of the stiff sheets I'm lying on. The warm sunlight we lay under chills into the hospital smells that surround me now. Our laughter is replaced by the drones and beeps and buzzes of monitors.

This time when I open my eyes, I feel less shock and amazement that I have returned from the dead. I expected I would. What confidence one needs in their medical caretaker to make that assumption. Wow.

I am back.

I have succeeded. I am not grateful to be alive. I am satisfied with a job well done. This is not a Thank You, Jesus moment. It is a Mission Accomplished one.

No. Not yet. I have to sketch.

The foyer. My mother. Her eyes. The cop's forearms. His muscular back. The stack of mail. The closed front door. My mother's nervous body language. I have to get everything down immediately.

Cordoba left pencils and a brand-new sketch pad on the table next to my bed. I force my brittle muscles to grab the tools and start drawing a wide picture of the scene. The master shot. I'll use this to trigger myself to remember more details as the day gets later. I can't feel some of my fingers, so it takes longer than I hoped.

I'm starving and I feel hung-over, although that's impossible. Being dead is a great way to stop drinking.

I finish a rough of the master shot and move next to my mother's eyes. Furtive. Frantic. Needy.

Wait.

I waste a few seconds checking my body for missing organs. I feel much better than the last time. No stitches. No missing limbs. Still have two eyes. Feels like she kept her part of the bargain.

Except for the sex. What was that?

Cordoba humped me like a truck stop whore as I was dying and probably for a while afterward. It was preplanned. She was ready with the hard-on medicine and timed it to perfection. Better to ask forgiveness than permission, I guess. I already know I want her to kill me again so the issue has to be addressed. Or does it? Do I really care what happens to the bag of tissue that hosts my mind and gets me from place to place? Argue it all you want, but I'm not offended. No, not at all.

The cop put his hand on my mother's shoulder. I was in the room and they know I saw it happen. I sketch the basics of the gesture and wonder what the point was. A practiced move calculated to reassure a hysterical housewife. An over-familiar touch. A random act. It was either empathetic or shameless or meaningless.

I readjust myself and feel a little something on my chest. Peeking inside the gown she put me in I see rounded rectangles of burn marks on my chest. About the size of defibrillator paddles. Looks like I was dead dead. Maybe this wasn't the easiest procedure ever performed. But whatever. Here I am.

My mother had a bruise on her eye, but that was not why she called the cops. It was healing. She had no fresh injuries. Only residual panic. She had to know I could hear what she was saying.

Where is Cordoba anyway? Isn't one of these monitors letting her know I'm up and conscious?

I'm almost done with sketches. Drawing the cop's forearms is easy although I'm not sure why I would ever need them. But everything goes down. Everything. Except his face. I couldn't hang on long enough to see his god damn face.

Cordoba walks in. She's unimpressed that I'm awake. Maybe one of those monitors did let her know. I have no idea what any of them do. She checks the one closest to me and I don't know by her reaction what it tells her.

—How are you feeling?

Business as usual. Not that I expect a high-five, but she is one cold fish. She checks my vitals. I'm perfect or at death's door. She doesn't tell me which.

—I feel great, relatively.

Although, I have paddle burns on my chest. How close was I?

—Did you have any trouble bringing me back?

Cordoba ignores the question and places a fresh syringe and more meds on the tray next to the bed. Magic medicine. Looks like she's down for another round as well. Alright, let's say there was no trouble. Which leaves us with the one question I can't resist asking.

—The sex. Right when I died. What was that?

Her hair is once again pulled back into a tight ponytail and she looks at me so very evenly. Like the predator that she is. It's either anger or embarrassment. No, it's neither. I wonder if she feels emotions at all. She waits for me to withdraw the question. I won't.

—That's why you lost your license.

—That was a consideration, yes.

Unapologetic. Just the facts. Take it or leave it.

—So what happens next time I die?

—Do you need to die again?

—I do.

Finally, she moves her eyes away from mine to the syringe.

—Come back in two days.

When her eyes come back to meet mine again, they're dead. Cold. Lifeless. It's time for me to leave.

71

I'm still hungry and the sunlight is killing my eyes.

I've never been this sensitive. The street is crowded and I know people are giving me a wide berth as I make my way uptown. I'm trying to go unnoticed, but that's not going to happen. Even among the homeless around here, I stand out. Unstable has its own distinct aura.

My sketches are rolled up under my left arm and I've got the syringes locked in a death grip in my right hand. I want to go start the recovery process as soon as possible, but if I don't eat I might not make it back to my apartment.

I sell my watch at a pawn shop I noticed on the way over. Lisa paid a little more than eight grand for it one Christmas. I never understood the extravagance but it seemed to be meaningful to her so I kept the watch. Never took it off. She had it engraved with our initials separated by a plus sign over the phrase *Truly, madly, deeply*. I believe at the time it was true.

The greasy little broker gives me four hundred. We both know he's ripping me off, so he pretends to be doing me a favor and tells me I'm lucky he doesn't call the cops. In the reflection of the two-way glass behind him, I see that my hair is now completely gray. I look twenty years older than when I started this mishigas.

Truly, madly, deeply. Noticeably absent from the phrase was the word forever.

There's a diner across the street. I go in and order three breakfasts. The place is empty and I can't resist unrolling the sketches and spreading them out across my table and the two that flank it.

My mother.

The cop.

I don't know what else to do. He's not leaving me any choice.

What was my father doing that was so bad the cops had to set up some secret plan with my mother? Domestic violence doesn't usually merit a full covert operation. Her eyes stare back at me but don't answer. They never answer.

My food arrives and I eat it like the starving pig that I am. I've never tasted food this good. I don't know if the illegal immigrant in the back happens to be the best cook in the world or this is a byproduct of being brought back to life. Doesn't matter. I contemplate a fourth breakfast but I'll vomit if I do and fuck if I'm wasting what little money I have like that. I can't move fast enough to skip out, so I pay the check, screw the waitress on the tip, and leave.

I don't get ten steps out the door before I know I'm being followed. Same feeling I had before only stronger. I stop.

Nothing.

There's nothing behind me. Even with my oversensitive eyes, I can see there's no one creeping up on me. No whistling simpletons. No bogeymen. Nothing. WTF?

When I turn back toward my home, I'm met with the self-satisfied smirk of the exact motherfucker I thought might be following me. Standing there waiting for me. About six inches from my face. Goose, the mustache man. Smiling like the dickhead that he is.

—Who are you?

Did Harry send him to watch me? Could he be an old friend of Lisa's? Do I owe him money? What could he possibly want from a bottomed-out loser?

—Who. Are. You.

He doesn't answer me, of course. Just stands there with that shit-eating grin stretched across his face. I don't know how he snuck up on me, but here we are.

He head butts me before I can make a move. Fucking head butts me right in the nose. Blood is pouring out my nostrils and past my hand as if I hadn't even raised it.

I back away from him as I try to balance not getting blood on my drawings with not losing control of the meds in my pocket with figuring out why I'm being attacked by a stranger.

He's grinning even wider as he watches me suffer. I think he laughs to himself. It must be going better than he hoped. Congratulations, pal.

I gather myself and throw a punch, landing a beaut of a right cross on his cheek. He shakes it off like it's nothing. Didn't feel it. Am I that weak or is he that strong?

He takes a step closer and grabs my left wrist, the arm with the drawings tucked under it. I fight to keep my elbow chicken-winged against my side but he's stronger than I am. Stronger than anyone I've ever met. The drawings drop to the ground and I do my best not to step on them. I can still feel my meds in my pocket. Why did I take my hand off of them? He plants a foot firmly on my sketches and yanks me toward him.

He head butts me again on my forehead and it hurts worse than the first one. Is he getting stronger? My knees buckle and I drop but not all the way to the ground. I can't. Goose holds me up by the wrist high enough to punch me in the face several times.

He's pounding me. I remember when I used to like this kind of thing. There was nothing like a good beat down to take the edge off. Release a little stress. It gave me such clarity. As he takes his fist back again, I realize I'm not getting the same kind of thrill this time. No sharp pang of anticipation before his knuckles meet the thin flesh covering the border of my eye socket. Is that because I didn't provoke it or because what I've been up to is so much more dangerous than being pounded into raw meat? I think I've desensitized myself to this level of danger. It's boring. But I know I've got to go through it. How is Goose not breaking his hand on my face? Shouldn't he at least be getting tired by now? He's enjoying this. Truly, madly, deeply.

I hear a bystander say *What's he doing?* and another calls out something that sounds like *Do you need some help?* I can't answer. My mouth is full of blood and I'm having trouble focusing my eyes.

Finally, Goose is kind enough to let me drop the ground. I manage to not land on my meds by turning to the side and letting my bony hip absorb the brunt of the fall. Goose takes the opportunity to launch a few kicks into my stomach.

How are there no cops here by now? I've gotten a summons for walking out of a bar to smoke a cigarette with a drink in my hand. And there are no cops around when this is going down? No good Samaritans with martial arts training? No one's even yelling at Goose to stop. Can't anyone on this street see that I'm getting mugged or whatever this is? The crowd that has gathered to watch this beat down is not reacting the way I would expect. No one is horrified at the senseless violence taking place fifteen feet away from them. One guy even looks sort of amused. Like he might post it on YouTube.

Goose offers no explanation for the attack. And he's so efficient with his blows. This can't have gone on longer than forty-five seconds. I've been reduced to a cowering sack of cuts and bruises in under a minute. But he hasn't said a word.

This is so wrong. If I'm going to die for real, I want it on my own terms.

And then it's over. By the time I notice he has stopped kicking me, Goose is ambling down the street as if nothing ever happened. And whistling. No one even looks at him as he passes. Me, they never take their eyes off of, fascinated. The bloody pile of human. I presume this is because, as ragged as I was before the beating, I must look exponentially worse now. Like I might die right in front of them and they don't want to be distracted for a second. How often do you have the opportunity to see something like this? Maybe they think I live on this sidewalk. That I'm used to this. That I deserve it.

Finally, someone says they're calling for an ambulance and my blood starts pumping again. I don't need a doctor. I have a doctor. And I'm not going to a hospital. I guarantee what I've got in my pocket will help me far more than whatever they cook up for me in the psychiatric department. My shaky hand digs around and pulls out the meds. They're still intact. How the fuck did my knuckles get so bloody? I thought I only got one punch in.

I struggle to my feet, gather up my sketches, which are now blood-streaked and trampled with boot prints. One of my teeth lies on the ground but I don't pick it up. I'm gone before the ambulance arrives. If it ever came.

72

If Lisa were still talking to me and happened to be here right now, she'd have plenty to say on the subject.

The layout of the drawings. The order. A better way to attach them to the wall, perhaps. I'm using tape but it doesn't hold great on brick. It's good enough.

I put the new drawings up next to the old ones. The order doesn't make much sense, but every time I reorder them, they make less and less sense. Which came first and what followed what is a complete mystery. Most likely Forearm Cop showed up after one of the big fights but maybe not. How the fuck am I going to keep this up? There are so many gaps to fill in.

My tongue is a little swollen and I have a craving to eat ice and I think dirt, as well. Those are symptoms of anemia. Lack of iron in my red blood cells. Or lack of red blood cells. Makes sense. My marrow has been taxed beyond belief. The recuperation I'm forcing on myself must be the equivalent of a turbo growth spurt. You can only run an engine so fast for so long before something breaks down. Looks like we're starting with anemia. Oh well.

If Lisa were talking to me she'd notice that my sketches are now taking up a good two thirds of my (our) wall. It's an impressive sight if you know their origins. But she wouldn't know the origins. I never told her. She might offer some suggestions on order or aesthetics, but she'd be guessing as much as I am.

Eventually, she would tell me enough with the rearranging. I could do this for hours but I have to maintain my priorities. I have some recovering to do. Lisa was good like that. Recovery means more memories. More memories means answers. I get my gallon of water ready and fill my syringe up.

BOOM! BOOM! BOOM!

Someone pounds on my door. I limped home. Looking back on it I must have left a trail of blood. Easy enough to follow if you were the police or EMTs who showed up at the scene of my beating. Or if you're Goose, come to finish the job. But he already knows where I live. If it is that smiling fuck, I can do nothing to stop him once he gets past the locks. I'm weak and I'm tired and I'll die in my living room and no one will know until the neighbors complain about the smell. No reviving. No way back from The White.

BOOM! BOOM! BOOM!

If it were the cops, they would have identified themselves by now. It's not the cops. Great. Now, this is where Lisa and I would differ. She would tell me I deserve this. Running around like a madman. You make your own fate.

The pounding isn't strong enough to break down the door, but maybe he's not trying that hard. How long is he willing to wait? Why follow me home to finish me off? He didn't seem to care about witnesses. Why not kill me on the sidewalk? And who the fuck is this guy? Why decide to torture me all of a sudden? I'm just a guy trying to kill himself over and over and minding my own business. God damn it's annoying.

—Christian!

Through the door. It's Ella. Oh, Lisa would have a fucking mouthful to say about this. Like don't answer the door. And it's none of her business. And shut the fuck up.

BOOM! BOOM! BOOM!

—Christian, open the door. I can hear you moving around in there.

It is her business and it has been for a long time. It was her business just like it was mine. Ella's angry. She's going to yell for a while, I can already tell. But I need her so I unlock the door.

It's barely open before she throws a wad of papers in my face and storms in. It's the copies of the drawings I shoved through her mail slot in my face. Good, she got them.

—What were you thinking?

If Lisa were here I wonder if she would defend me. I like to think she would jump in front of me and tell Ella she's handling this completely the wrong way. What is needed here is compassion and understanding on her part. Not anger. I've got enough of that for all of us.

—What is wrong with you?

If I started to explain she wouldn't listen. Ella needs to yell. It's her process, like dying is mine. I only wish her timing were a tad better. I'm not up for drama right now. My right eye is swollen shut and I'm having trouble breathing through my nose. Ella turns to face me. Steaming.

It hits her. How bad I look.

—Oh god. What happened?

No way around this. I haven't looked too closely lately but I'm sure my face has aged to match my gray hair. And, there's the missing teeth. Also, my anemia is making me even paler than I would be from dying so often. I'm only five years older than her, but if you asked a stranger, they might guess we were father and daughter. At least it softens her up a bit.

—I'm okay.

I can see Ella making the internal choice to take care of herself and her family before she helps me.

—Look, I get that you're having a tough time, Christian. But I told you I'm not getting involved in whatever chaos you've got going on. You've got to stop sneaking around and causing trouble.

At this point Lisa might tell me she told me so. She told me I should have never gone to the dog fights or Ella's house. She told me so.

—What am I supposed to tell the kids about those horrible drawings? They were scared. And now I have to lie to Tim about why you would leave those for me. I'm not interested in telling Tim or anyone else for that matter what happened. It was thirty fucking years ago, Christian.

My loft must smell awful. I have cleaned none of my messes up for weeks. My voice sounds like a bad Sam Eliot impression.

—Christian? What are you doing?

—I'm so close to so many answers.

I indicate to the wall of drawings and it's clear that she didn't notice them when she walked in. She looks at my massive, sloppy, homemade shrine.

—What is this?

—Do you remember any of this? Does this trigger anything? You were there for some of these.

—Christian—

—What's missing? What am I missing? I can go back but I have to know what to look for.

—Go back where? Where are these coming from? What are they supposed to be? Why are you doing this?

I can't explain to her how I'm getting them. The effort would be too much. She's back to her comfort zone of borderline hysterical and I do not have the stamina. My head is throbbing. All I can do is beg.

—Ella, look closely. Tell me what you see. Tell me what this reminds you of.

She looks. Ella takes a step back to stare at the wall. She takes it all in. A few moments in, she looks over to me and then back to the wall. Her eyes well up and she tries unsuccessfully to blink back tears.

—Christian, you need help.

—Yes, from you.

—Yes, from me. I will help you find the professionals who can help you.

—I've been to them. I have better people. What I need now is your mind. Your memories. Tell me what all this means.

She marches over to the wall and rips a row of sketches down. And then another. I'm dumbfounded. I move toward her as fast as I can, but by the time I can grab her wrist, she's got a dozen more drawings down, crumpled at her feet.

—What are you doing!

I lean my entire body into moving her away from the wall. She could fight harder but she doesn't. Finally, she stops resisting entirely.

—You need help.

She's backing away from me toward the door, forgetting she's still got a sketch of our mother in her hand. The one that says *Why won't he leave me alone?*

Ella gets to the front door and when she realizes she's holding the drawing, she drops it like it was on fire. Like she suddenly wants a shower.

—You need help.

The struggle re-aggravated my most recent injuries and her voice is a knife in my eye.

Lisa would tell me to take her help. That despite everything, Ella is my best bet. That I should curl up on the floor and let her wait with me until someone comes to take me away to a facility with plenty of oxytocin, dopamine, norepinephrine, and phenylethylamine and the orderlies big enough to make me swallow them.

—Just try, Ella. Try to remember.

Ella cries harder. She turns and walks out without closing the door. I can hear her sobbing all the way down the stairs.

Fine then. I'll do it myself.

—FUCK OFF!

Oh, Lisa would have had a lot to say about all of this.

I force myself to move across the room, shut the door, and lock it. If you're not with me, you're against me. I'm sweating by the time I get there and have to sit down to recover whatever energy is left in my body.

Seven minutes later, I tie off my right arm and jam a syringe into the big fat vein running through the middle. I've forgotten about Ella before the plunger is all the way down.

This is exactly what I needed.

Black.

73

*It's three months ago.

I'm on my way into work when that twat Michelle sees me on the street and looks awkward. Surprise, surprise, she doesn't want to see me or talk to me or acknowledge my existence. But she approaches me anyway. Makes eye contact with me, for Christ's sake.

Fuck, she's gonna yell at me about all the phone calls. The point was to get Lisa's attention not to have a sit down with her BFF. So, what are my options? Tell her to piss off and keep moving? No good. That'll get right back to Lisa and we'll be three steps back. Listen patiently and nod? I know she'll use that insanely condescending voice and I'll feel like vomiting, but that's probably the best play. The listening, not the vomiting. Alright, bitch. Bring it on.

Michelle walks right up to me and puts on a face that's equal parts disgust and sympathy. Like I said, always with the condescension. She offers her condolences and I think she's being funny or sarcastic or something.

—If there's anything I can do . . .

If there's anything you can do? What would you do for me? You can go fuck yourself to start.

Wait.

It dawns on me that she knows something I don't. It dawns on her about the same time.

Manhattan is so fucking loud.

—Christian, I thought Lisa's mother called you.

—Why would she call me?

She starts talking but I already know what she's going to tell me. Just like I knew Dana would bring Lisa to my apartment even though I never invited her. Just like I knew I shouldn't marry her even though I had to. I knew what Michelle was going to tell me and as much as I wanted to not hear it or run away or clamp my hand over her fat mouth I did nothing. Nothing. And her words spilled out all over me and I heard them.

Lisa is gone. Gone. Gone. Gone.

I turn and walk away. Michelle might still be talking.

The details filter in through my fog as I float down the sidewalk. Lisa stepped off a curb. A bus didn't stop. There was a head injury. Nothing they could do. Happens every day. Everyone is so sorry. It was in the *Post*.

No wonder she wasn't calling me back.

74

The Black releases me after two intense days.

I wake up naked in my own filth once again. The water bottle is empty and across the room, this time crushed flat. The clothes I was wearing have been thrown out an open window. The chairs from my dining table are scattered across the floor. This appears to be the result of having been stacked and knocked over. Every dish and glass in my kitchen is broken and on the floor. My front door is still locked from the inside. I remember nothing. It's early afternoon.

I take a quick inventory of my body. A few scratch marks. An impression of my teeth still visible on my wrist and starting to bruise. My thumbnails have been pulled out. I feel thinner.

Beyond that, I am fantastic.

I feel like a new man. Refurbished. I might even be energetic. My reflection in the bathroom mirrors lacks any of the deep cuts and hideous disfigurements I was given during the beating forty-eight hours ago. As if it had never happened.

I run my hand through my hair and a clump of it comes out easily. And then another. I shower and the water finishes the job, washing away whatever was left on my scalp. My eyebrows wipe away. My pubic hair brushes off completely. My hair clogs the drain and if I cared whether or not the tub emptied I would clear it. I am now hairless.

I air dry standing in front of my drawings, half of which are still strewn across the floor. Staring at them. Trying to upload the arrangement into my consciousness as a whole. A shabby representation of the unfinished masterpiece constructed in a medium in which I alone work. There must be a hundred sketches. I cannot take my eyes off of them.

My father yelling.

My mother crying.

The purse.

The washing machine.

The cop's forearms.

The stoop.

The tension.

The fat cop.

I know I'm right about this.

Outside, my clothes are all pretty close together. I must have thrown them out fairly recently since this is New York and you can't leave anything of any value on the sidewalk without someone walking away with it. People watch as I go from naked to dressed in my discarded clothes right there in the open, but no one says anything.

I walk straight over toward Cordoba's office, eating three breakfast burritos on the way. I can feel my stomach ripping the food apart, breaking it down and shipping it out to the cells who so desperately need it. My metabolism is revved. Redlining. The closer I get the better I feel. As if the magic meds took me so far down the rabbit hole I'm still slingshotting back up even now. I'm riding the momentum of recovery. Flying. I internalize the feeling and savor the tingle racing around the inside crown of my head. My brain is dancing. I don't even want a drink. I haven't been able to say that for years. Christ, I'm high on life. And I can't wait to die again.

Approaching Cordoba's building, I remind myself that I'm that much closer to being whole again. That much closer to realizing the potential Lisa saw in me. I'm clearing out roadblocks and I'll never again be unavailable. I'm evolving.

I know a lot of this is mania but why can't I make it true? Why can't I live the dream? This is the kind of transformation that brings people back together forever.

Her front door lock is broken. The door is slightly ajar.

Before I can process this, I run head on into Goose's smirking face.

He's on his way out of her building and in what would appear to be a rush but stops when he realizes who I am. That fucking grin. And me fully recovered. I force myself to breathe evenly. Maybe this is a good thing. Maybe this is one more thing my new self can check off his to do list, huh? I'm going to kill this piece of shit and this time it'll be a fair fight.

—What are you doing here?

Goose smiles a little broader as if he knows I'm ready to throw down. He jerks forward enough to make me think he's throwing a punch and I don't flinch one iota. He shrugs it off with a chuckle but I know he's recalculating his attack plan.

Why would he be in Cordoba's building? Is he a patient? Could he possibly be seeing her as well? For what? What are the chances that the two of us would be using the same underground doctor regardless of the reason?

Unless he's not a patient. Unless he followed me here when I came before.

To do what? Who even knows what's going on in this building besides me and her? My anger and aggression and confidence has quickly curdled into a whirling eddy of questions and I have almost forgotten that I intend to murder the fucknut in front of me.

Goose tires of waiting for me to make a move. He shakes his head, clucks his tongue, and walks past me, bumping my shoulder as he goes. Like I'm not even worth the effort. The option to follow him is wide open. Run after him. Tackle him. Beat him.

But I'm right here. I'm ready to die. That's what I need to be doing. I need to get to Cordoba.

Oh shit.

Cordoba.

I hit the stairs running and take them two at a time. Her front door is wide open and I can smell the blood before I get into the office. Inside the stark front room, Cordoba lies sprawled across the couch with her head turned awkwardly enough that I know for sure she's dead. My shoulder hits the doorframe as I walk backwards without even realizing it. I'm repulsed but I can't stop staring. Her neck is broken and both eyes have syringes jammed into them. Her legs are crossed at the ankles and her arms are spread wide as if she were going to hug me for the first time. She has been posed. This is what I get for being optimistic.

He killed her.

He knew how important she was to me and he came up here and killed her. Why her and not me when he had the chance? What's the point? To torture me? Squash any chance I have at rebuilding myself? Imprison me in my own life? I was so close to picking the lock and now that's over.

I'll never be brought back again.

I have nothing. I have nothing and nobody and I'll die alone and ignorant and it won't be long from now.

I'm dead already.

There's nothing left for me. Cordoba was the last friend I had in the world. I know friend is the wrong word. Accomplice, maybe. Either way, she was it. Ella might as well be a stranger for all the honest emotional interaction she'll allow herself with me and I've done such an admirable job of alienating myself from anyone else who ever showed me the smallest kindness that I am a self-made social outcast. I knew Cordoba for only days but I feel even emptier now that she's gone. I should call the police or see if she has a next of kin that should be notified, but she's dead and neither of those two actions will bring her back. Besides, I know she was alone like me. Dead like me.

Cordoba's bloody, syringe filled eyes stare up at the ceiling. I follow the gaze to see that written in blood, I assume shot from the syringes before using them to defile her face, is a message. To me. *Happy now?*

Where is he?

Where is that fucker who thinks I will not fight back?

I'm still flying from the magic meds and feel like I could tear an ox in half. The buzz in my head is forcing euphoria on me. Cordoba lying there with needles in her eyes is infusing this internal rapture with shrill, shooting adrenaline streaks of horror. They're feeding on each other. One amplifying the other. The realization that I am out of options fuels my absentee gunmetal gray cloud of depression to return with a vengeance, roiling and churning on top of everything else. Medically induced happiness steeped in profound shock and top notes of suicidal tendencies. My new base line.

75

(Sigh)

The saddest part is that this is entirely our man's fault.

Every tragic turn of this hopeless tale has been effected by the old boy's own clumsy hand. Every heartrending abomination of his recent past can be traced directly to his own actions. The inveterate self-saboteur's predicament is bleak at best and it is plain to even the dimmest of outsiders that his best next action would be to resign himself to alerting the authorities and accepting his share of whatever blame is to be doled out. And naturally, a commitment to a hospital or mental facility is in order as well.

But, as you must already know, he will do neither.

His state of mind is not one of acceptance or contrition or supplication, but rather revenge. He has suffered provocation beyond endurance. There are no degrees of emotion involved. His perspective is pure and undistracted. The incandescent rage of indignation boils over and our man rejiggers his agenda accordingly. A grievous sacrilege must be avenged. Beyond that, there is no further thought.

He calms himself, if only to focus harder on what he will do next. His eyes scan the room one last time, not for sentimental reasons, but to soak in fully the details of Cordoba's untimely demise. He nods, now fully realized in his murderous state of grace. Calmly, he exits the good doctor's office and moves down the stairs, gaining momentum as he goes. By the time he crosses the threshold of the building, he is running at full speed, and you would be well advised to steer clear of him. Collateral damage is no concern to our man.

Pity, really. There was a time when the old boy held promise as a husband, as a lawyer, as a human. Not so, anymore. Not so at all.

And now there is nothing left but to congratulate our man on his previous accomplishments and bid the malignant whelp Godspeed in what is left of his disquieting adventure.

Best of luck, old boy.

76

*It's three months ago.

I'm alone.

I stand in a cemetery about thirty yards away from the funeral Lisa's family has arranged for her. I know most of the people sitting around the grave. They don't know I'm there. Or they do and they're ignoring me.

Someone is talking. It must be the rabbi. I recognize the voice. Same guy who married us. The only person here who can't hear him is Lisa. She went black. Gone. They're all sitting around an empty vessel.

Lisa once told me she'd prefer that no fuss be made over her body when she died. Burn it. Donate it. Toss it. Whatever. I know she told her mother the same thing, but here we are with what I'm assuming is an expensive casket and a grave with a stunning view of Southern Philadelphia that must have cost plenty. What a waste.

Someone notices me, points me out to Lisa's mother. They whisper together and shake their heads. They're wondering why I'm standing out here. I don't know if they think I'm being disrespectful for staying this far away or getting this close.

I turn and walk away like it never happened.

77

*It's two months ago.

The doors close.

I'm sitting on the subway at the beginning of what I know will be at least a four-hour ride to nowhere. I know because I've done it every night for the last eight nights.

I'm staring at a secretary who's knitting fingerless gloves for someone she cares about and wearing her riding-the-subway-home shoes when it finally hits me that Lisa is never coming back to me. I can't explain the logic behind holding out hope this long but there it is, newly shattered on the floor in front of me.

Okay, then.

I stand up and walk out of the car and into the next car and then the next and then the next. I hate when other people change cars when the subway isn't too full. I guess their point is to simply keep moving. I know that's my point.

The last thing she said to me was that sometimes things in life don't work out and that we have to accept that. Worst philosophy ever. Things could have worked out. Somehow.

I get to the end of the train and turn around. There are other people in the car. A nanny with her four-year-old charge. An Asian couple. A family of German tourists blabbering about how to get to Ground Zero. There's a teenage boy by one of the doors. Standing there with his backpack and his earbuds and his life potential.

The train comes to a stop. As the doors open I make sure to bump the kid's shoulder good and strong. He's relaxed and slack and has one of those bodies that I can already tell has to be beat a lot to feel anything. Like melted rubber.

He doesn't react the way I want him to so I shove his soft shoulder. Finally, the little turd reacts.

—Yo, what the fuck?

I swat his iPhone out of his hands. It hits the floor and we both know it's broken. No more gangsta rap tonight, Junior.

He swings and I lean into it making sure his fist hits me square between the eyes. This generation is so entitled they can't even punch without a little help.

Perfect. I see black for a heartbeat and then my vision comes racing back, clearer than ever.

But I don't fall over or pass out like he's seen in so many movies, which scares the little shit. He starts backing off and it scares him worse that I move toward him. He backs up faster and faster, turning his hips to half run with his face still watching me. Finally, he turns all the way and bolts toward the exit. I want another fist in my face, maybe two or three, but it looks like that's not happening.

He's gone and now it's just me and a few stragglers who watched the whole thing go down from a safe distance away.

Lisa's never coming back. I know that now.

78

I practically break the door off of its hinges when I hit the sidewalk outside Cordoba's building.

I'm running. I have energy to burn. He couldn't have gotten far unless I was in there for longer than I think. Anything's possible. It felt like sixty seconds, but it might have been an hour.

Up Essex. It's not crowded and I can see to the end of the block. I've lost all my hair, but my vision is amazing. He's not here.

Left on Hester. Nothing.

Up Orchard. Where is this shitstain?

And then I stop. If I keep chasing him, I'll never catch him. But I know how to find him.

I turn and I casually walk back the way I came. Come and get me. It's not long before I know I'm being followed. I feel it. I keep going another half block to make sure and then I turn into an alley between a Chinese restaurant and a thrift store. And I stop.

When I turn around, he's there. The Cheshire cat of my newfound nightmare. Grinning like it was all his idea in the first place.

Hi, Goose.

There's no discussion this time. I swing away and land a right cross on his jaw. Who's strong now, asshole? I follow that with a left to his nose that has to hurt. His head is jerking back and forth with the punches but he's not dropping. He raises his eyebrows and makes his mouth an O to taunt me. Mock fear.

I swing my right hand and this time I put some stank on it. It lands squarely on his temple and he staggers back. This feels good. Better than it should. I'm on the other end of the beating for once and I'm getting a rush like I've never had.

Or is that a whoosh?

I throw another haymaker and connect with his cheek.

The whoosh grows from behind me. Holy shit. My eyes twitch and before I can blink it away the entire world wobbles, zigging and zagging back and forth before the whoosh is big enough to make everything go white.

The White.

I'm alone and pristine and content.

I'm not even dead and I'm here in The White. And I know what's coming. The whoosh is deafening and ramping up, impossibly loud yet unwaveringly reassuring. Something is on its way. I turn to see a single memory screaming toward me. It's so beautiful. If I had a body, I would be slobbering with anticipation as I wait for this big fat vision to run me over. It hits me and I'm there.

It's March of whatever year I was eight.

I've been here before. It's the recovered memory from the laundry room. I've already seen this. A fucking rerun? Are you kidding me?

I'm terrified. Yes, I remember this part. Why am I here?

I'm watching my mother cry as she stares at the locked door.

BOOM! BOOM! BOOM! I know that's my father and he's angry and my mother is scared.

—Let me in there, God dammit! Open this fucking door or I'll break it down!

BOOM! BOOM! BOOM!

—Open up!

She grabs the sides of her head and screams.

—Leave me alone! Why can't you leave me alone!

My mother curls up tighter on the floor and convulses with sobs. I'm watching. Helpless. Paralyzed.

She looks up at me. She talks to me like I'm an adult. A stranger.

—Why won't he leave me alone?

I have no answer for her. She sobs for a moment before pulling herself together and finishing what she started. Which was tying off to shoot up.

Oh.

My mother was a junkie. Oh, right.

Jesus.

BOOM! BOOM! BOOM!

—I'M COMING IN THERE!

She wraps a belt that looks like it would fit a boy about my age around her arm, yanks it with her teeth, and pumps her fist. I think it's me she's talking to through gritted teeth, but who knows.

—It's none of his business. He can't tell me what to do.

She flicks a lighter under a spoon and then sucks its contents up with a syringe in a practiced move.

Once the needle is in her arm and the plunger is down, she collapses in a triumphant slouch.

—It's my life. I . . . can do . . .

And she's out.

The door crashes open and my father's silhouette stands over us both. He's too late, once again. His anger is of no use now and he releases it.

—Christian?

He scoops me up and carries me out, leaving her slumped over behind us.

The memory takes on a life of its own, filling itself in on the front and back of what I have already discovered. Flowering and blossoming of its own accord into a more detailed entry now engraved in my consciousness. I know this isn't the first time I've seen her shoot up. I know that every time she does it, it's the scariest thing ever. I'm afraid, every time, she's not going to wake up. I know he's going to put me to bed. I know when I wake up in the morning he'll still be sitting at my side. I know that she'll still be there on the floor.

I'm eight and I'm terrified.

I'm back.

I'm out of The White and have no idea how long I've been out. I'm standing in the alley still holding Goose by the collar. He's on his knees enjoying this. I am empty of all emotion except gratitude. Gratitude for this new understanding. Gratitude that I can channel rage into action. Gratitude that I still have this cocksucker in my hot little hand.

I think Arnold Rosen would agree that I've had a breakthrough.

My mother was a junkie. Thirty-eight years I held her up like a saint. A victim. A martyr. A role model I knew nothing about.

Nope.

She was a stone addict right in front of my eyes. Even through my anger, there's a tinge of residual eight-year-old terror. Fuck her.

I am in control.

I look down at the blood-streaked teeth smiling back up at me. I will take what I need.

I punch Goose in his right eye as hard as I can and the whoosh comes even faster this time.

The White.

But only for a second. By the time I realize I'm here, a memory is bearing down on me.

It hits me and I'm there.

Brooklyn.

My home.

I'm eight.

This is the purse memory. My mother and father screaming at each other in the kitchen. The tension. Things have been getting worse. He's so angry.

—I've had enough of your shit!

—Stop trying to control me!

He grabs her purse. She fights for it. I'm trembling.

The memory flowers like the last one and I know it's a month after my last memory and that soon my father will disappear from my life for days because my mother will take us to a hotel to hide from him and get high. I know I'm praying to god that he'll stop fighting and take me and Ella away to somewhere else. Anywhere else. I've got to get away from this place.

—I want that money!

—No!

My sister is crying, but I do nothing.

—I am done fucking around! Give it to me!

My father yanks the purse away from her, knocking my mother down. She claws after him.

—NOOOO!

My father yanks out her wallet, takes all the cash and credit cards, and heads for the back door.

She collapses.

—What about my medicine?!

She curls up in the corner and howls. I turn to see that Ella has run to her room to do the same.

My father turns around to quietly explain her situation to her for the millionth time.

—It's not medicine. You're not sick. You're an addict. You promised me you'd quit and you're worse than ever. You're a liar and you're disgusting.

He looks at me.

—Come on.

I'm back.

In the alley. I'm holding Goose loosely but he's not going anywhere. Honestly, I'm kind of surprised he can muster a sneer but maybe he can't help himself.

You're a liar and you're disgusting.

I'm a liar and I'm disgusting.

I've been disgusting for a long time.

Goose's eyes are half closed, but he won't take them off me.

—'Bout fucking time.

Yeah. He's right. It is about fucking time.

I reel back and throw my clenched right fist at his nose.

The White.

The whoosh.

Another memory.

I'm home in Brooklyn.

This is the one where I watch my mother and the cop with the forearms. She looks from the cop to me and back to the cop. She's jumpy.

—I don't know what else to do. He's not leaving me any choice.

As the memory flowers, I remember being told to stand here by my mother after I was promised either ice cream or not getting beaten later on. She sent Ella to her room. I'm terrified and I remember waiting here alone in the dark when my mother answered the door. She never asked who it was so she must have been expecting the man standing in the room with her now. She wanted me to meet him. Told me I would like him. He's a nice policeman. The cop with the forearms.

She looks at me and back to him.

My mother's dress.

The mail piled up next to the front door.

Ella's toys in the hallway.

The broken chain lock on the front door.

The four-day-old bruise on my mother's eye.

The cop puts his hand on my mother's shoulder.

—I understand.

He pauses for a second.

—Will he be home anytime soon?

My mother shakes her head no.

I'm terrified and I don't know why. Where is Ella? I wish she were here so I could take care of her.

The cop turns to look my way and I recognize that face. It's the man I am currently beating the shit out of.

—No. He's out for the night.

Goose smiles. Practically licks his lips.

—Then I'm in for an hour.

He pulls a small baggie of white powder from his pocket and hands it to my mother without looking at her. Too focused on me.

My flowering memory tells me that in a few moments my mother will introduce him to me with the phony title of uncle.

The alley.

Goose.

I don't waste a millisecond. I punch this fucker in his smug face before he can so much as giggle at me.

The White.

The whoosh.

Oh.

This is a new one.

Brooklyn.

I'm eight.

My bedroom.

The flowering tells me this is a week after the last memory.

I'm trembling. The door is closed and I know it is locked because I know my mother made sure to lock it. The only light in the room is the nightlight next to my dresser. My mother sits on my bed, tucking me in.

No, she's pulling the covers back.

I recognize the burning sensation in the back of my head as a very specific type of fear. I'm clutching my favorite bedtime book. I know she's got another baggie in her front pocket. She seems to want to get things moving.

—Mommy, I'm scared.

She slides the book I'm hugging to my chest out from my hands and holds it as if she were going to read it. She's not.

—I know, sweetie. But everything is going to be fine. Your uncle just wants to show you how much he loves you. And this time keep quiet. You don't want to wake your sister.

I want to cry or scream or run or hit her but I know I've tried those things before and they've only made things worse. And begging is useless. I know this is going to hurt like fuck but I have to shut down and deal with it. I wish it would end but maybe this happens in every home to every eight-year-old.

Footsteps stomp quickly down the hallway. The bedroom door bursts open, breaking the frame as it does, and light floods the room from the hallway. My father stands holding his service revolver. In this new light, I see Goose across the room, frozen in the act of taking off his pants. My father sees him as well but he doesn't look too surprised. More like disgusted. Goose's gun belt is laid neatly across a chair far enough away that we all know he'll be shot dead before he gets to it.

Doesn't matter.

My father swivels and points the gun at my mother.

—I begged you, Stephanie.

He pulls the trigger and I see my mother's brains leave the back of her head and coat the wall where my bulletin board hangs. She falls over on top of me, arms on either side.

My father deflates. His gun drops to the floor and he stares at what he has done. Young Goose yanks his pants up, scrambles for his gun, and scurries past my father, who does nothing to stop him.

I know all of this because I heard my father's gun hit the carpet and Goose's belt jingle and his clothes rustle and his footsteps rush out the door and down the stairs. I can't see anything because my mother's body is blocking my sight and I'm too scared to move her.

The alley.

Goose lies below me, his eye swelling, blood seeping out the side of his mouth. I don't need to punch him again to figure out what my first recovered memory meant.

My father sitting in the back of the squad car. Watching me. Knowing he gave me my life back. His actions had to have been premeditated and more importantly, he knew what would happen to him after he acted.

Thank you, I said.

—She wasn't trying to save you. She was trying to sell your ass.

And there it is. A lifetime's worth of guilt turned on its head. An entire ingrained subconscious behavior pattern revealed as off target. Or worse, a waste of time.

I never wrote my father back.

I never let Lisa in.

I never gave myself a chance.

—I'm trying to figure out who was the better fuck. You or your mom?

Goose sounds like he has some life left in him, but only enough to remind me that he's still here and that I've got a little more work to do.

I hoist him back up by his throat in a vice grip and squeeze with all the strength I have. His eyes bug and he sputters blood across my face with his big, arrogant mouth.

I squeeze for my dead father and for my eight-year-old self and for my thirty-three-year-old sister. I'm squeezing hard enough that I know I must be crushing his larynx beyond the help of even New York's finest surgeons.

I squeeze like he is my mother.

The whoosh.

It's coming closer and closer the harder I squeeze and I know if I stop squeezing this fucker's neck, the whoosh will die so I force the muscles in my hands to contract more and more.

The whoosh grows and I realize that it's coming from down the street. I turn around to face the alley entrance in time to see a deluge of memories funneling in toward me. But this is different. They're not racing past me but straight at me, every single one. They hit me and I absorb them and I have room for all of them. There are so many but I can take them and understand them instantly. As if they were already there and only now waking up. I am being refilled. I am becoming whole. I'm manic with accomplishment and find that the harder I squeeze, the faster they come, so I redouble my efforts.

My third birthday party. Sitting in my second-grade class. Me as a five-year-old in front of the TV at home. Breast feeding. Learning to walk. It's all here.

I can feel his windpipe meeting his spine.

Learning to swim at seven. Reading aloud at six. Lying in bed with my father and mother. Playing catch with my father. Watching my mother feed baby Ella.

Goose claws at my face. Too late.

Listening to my mother tell my father she quit drinking.

Walking my mother upstairs after a visit to the doctor.

Watching my mother stare out the window for hours.

Standing in a filthy apartment while my mother scored.

Seeing my parents fight, knowing my mother is lying about what she's been doing.

Holding Ella while she sobs.

Goose is losing strength.

I have complete control over the entire collection in my library. I can fast forward, rewind, freeze frame.

Stickball in the street.

Finding my mother passed out on the kitchen floor for the first time. Christmas morning.

I am now in possession of the title and deed to my life free and clear.

Goose stops struggling. His arms fall to his side.

The memories speed up. They're coming so fast now they start to blend into one brilliant white light. Faster and the light grows to a brightness I can't take. Faster until there is nothing but white. Faster until I'm consumed by a flash of blinding light that engulfs me.

And then it's gone.

No light. No whoosh. No rushing memories. No Goose. I'm alone in the alley.

I know Goose was never here.

I know what needs to be done.

I know everything.

79

(Well, this complicates matters.)

The old boy has managed to complete his task of memory recoupment in the most inadvertent of manners and ahead of whatever arbitrary schedule he had set for himself.

Sadly, this freshly unearthed trove of treasure has not set him free from his self-imposed prison. Rather it has placed even more obstacles in his path. Now flush with childhood imagery and thrilling with the vigor new discoveries bring, our man is more befuddled than ever. Longstanding beliefs have been upended. Old emotions thrown into question. New wrinkles have been added to his road to reinvention.

Our man is determined to understand the significance of the events he is now aware of and arrange them in the correct and meaningful context, the Rosetta stone being the identity of the newest player in this confounding drama. Decoding the past is now predicated on unraveling the identity of the man whose neck he so recently held in his hands. This will take more time. More effort on top of what has already been so very draining.

Surely, this shift in gears is a huge mistake. But then all of this has been, hasn't it? And to what end? To rebuild himself as a healthier version of the man he was at one time resigned to be? To reconstruct himself as the man his wife would fall in love with all over again? To reincarnate himself as someone lovable who could not be left under any circumstances? It's too late for that, no? Far too late for that.

But try explaining to our man the realities of his situation. He'd never accept it, and, further, without his indulgent, Sisyphean mission, what has he left?

Nothing, I'm afraid.

His plan has morphed. What originally started as a quest for knowledge has interwoven itself with a pursuit of vengeance as well. And necessarily so, the delicacy of revenge serves as the irresistible temptation that a personality like his can burn as fuel for a very long time.

It can happen that fast. Our man has lost track of what is truly important. Forsaken the peace of forgiveness for the opportunity for retribution. In his mind lives the unshakeable belief that without completing the circle he thinks himself to be in, he will never be whole. Incapable of realizing his true potential. Alone. But the regrettable truth is that is exactly how the old boy will end up.

And sooner than he would like to believe.

80

I've explained the events of the day to Ella but I can see in her eyes she doesn't believe me. Not at all. What I'm telling her is impossible, and she's sick of my shit. Fine. But I know what I saw.

She hands me the photo album she's added to for the last twenty-five years. Pictures of my parents. Newspaper articles about the shooting. Letters from my father. This is her childhood. I collected nothing but the letters my father sent me and those I threw away once I thought he had stopped writing. Ella kept everything. And then she dug up so much more. She wasn't there for the shooting and everything that led up to it, so to her it was a fascinating story about two people she barely knew. Romantic, almost. I can only imagine the stories she made up to justify why she had to live with our idiot foster parents. She tried to talk to me about it when she was old enough but I had already repressed everything, so I mostly listened to her questions and said I didn't know. She asked the adults in our life and they told her what they thought was best.

Some truths were unavoidable.

Your father killed your mother.

Your father is in jail for life.

Your father killed himself.

Some could be bent and refinished and glossed over.

No one knows why he killed her.

Your father had a breakdown.

At one time they were very happy.

My father never spoke about that night. Not to me and as far as I can tell never to Ella. So she dug through archived newspapers and microfiche at the library and she talked to the cops who responded and she tracked down the EMTs who were there and when the Internet came around it only got worse. She lived to research and read and e-mail investigators and IM Dr. HackShag's widow and then research some more. For a while, she found herself caught up in the rabbit hole of conspiracy theories, but it only lasted for a few months, as it did nothing to further her understanding of one particular night. She reconstructed the evening and the events that led up to it as best she could, but it never amounted to more than a photo album that I have never taken the time to even open. Based on the questions she asked so many times, I knew it held nothing new for me.

Nothing until now.

I already know I'll find Goose in there. I just don't know what the context will be. It took her a good ten minutes to find the album while I waited on the front porch. Probably a good sign for her. She must have given up long ago and stashed it in the attic or basement or somewhere you put things you never want to see again but can't throw out.

—Christian, enough. Let's get you some help.

I flip through the book as she stares at what's left of me. She wouldn't let me in the house. We're standing on her front porch.

The front page of the *Post*.

The article from inside the paper that day.

My father's picture from the academy.

My mother's high school yearbook photo.

Their wedding picture.

How are all of these in the same album?

More articles on the murder.

A copy of the police report that tells me nothing I don't already know.

An article in which my father's partner is interviewed.

That's him.

Same mustache. Same cocky face.

Edward DeMare. Eddie.

I fucking knew it.

—I gotta go.

—Christian, let me drive you somewhere. There are places that will take you in today. Treat you. We'll pay for it. I'll talk to Tim.

It's thirty years later but I know where he is.

—Christian, please.

She touches my shoulder. I'm not having it. I hand Ella her album back and leave without thanking her.

Now I need a gun.

81

Flaco doesn't recognize me when I sit down next to him at the bar.

I can see in the mirror behind the tequila why he can't be blamed for it. It's a bit of a jarring realization to see how far I've come in so short a time.

From one perspective I have achieved everything I'd hoped and dreamed when I started this insane journey. I've seen things no man ever thought possible and I've done it several times. I won. Or seen from a different perspective, I've lost everything. Soon my health will fail me and, with my favorite moral-free doctor dead in her office, I no longer have a safety net. I'm choosing to see this glass half-full.

I have to convince Flaco I'm the guy who called him an hour ago. The same guy he met with a few weeks earlier, only now bald and missing teeth and looking way older than I should. It helps that I'm buying him beers, and whether he really recognizes me or not, what's important here is that he brought me a fully loaded Glock. He did.

I hand him what's left of the cash I got for my watch. A little over three hundred, I think. I don't need it anymore. If I'm understanding his god damn accent correctly, he's telling me the gun is stolen but clean, and if I don't get caught, that I should throw it in the river when I'm done. And, if I do get caught, I don't know him.

Fine.

82

*It's six weeks ago.

Harry is insisting I see a professional.

He feels strongly that self-medication is not the way to go in my case. He also thinks you have to nip these things in the bud or they can really get out of control. Mmm-hmm. Nip it, nip it, nip it. That is excellent advice, Harry.

He's speaking to me as a friend and it makes me sad to see him so human. His raw emotion is as touching as it is revolting.

I know he's right. He did it himself when Evelyn died. He was a wreck for months, drunk and useless. But look at him now.

The right way out of this is the most painful one. As always. If I want to heal, I need to hurt first. I need to be honest and vulnerable and do the work that so many people before me have done. I need to let go of the past and write my own future. Emotional rehab. Mental boot camp. Acting like a mature adult. I'll be a healthier person for it. He's right. He's so right.

I tell him I've started seeing a counselor. Brilliant guy. Works with people in my situation all the time. Really gets me. I've been to two sessions and I'm already starting to feel better. It's only the beginning, but I can see where it's going and I'm willing to do the work. I tell him I'm hopeful. I even volunteer a Jewish surname that I'm confident Harry won't check into and if he does, there's a good chance of there being a doctor with that same name somewhere in Manhattan.

Harry seems relieved and backs off a bit. He congratulates me on taking the first of many difficult steps and then we have that predictable awkward moment between men who have shared something personal beyond their historical friendship boundaries.

I excuse myself and leave the building to buy a pint of Austrian vodka in honor of Sigmund Freud. It's gone before I get to the bar in which I'll spend the rest of the night.

Nip that.

83

The high of recovery has dimmed a bit but I'm still humming along, even after five hours of standing around across the street from the front door of the sixth precinct station. My father's old home base.

I have done no research. I haven't called ahead. I did not check online. But I know in my gut that if this fucker is still alive, he's here. I know he's a lifer and I'm happy to wait for every shift change that happens from now until I drop dead.

Aside from the falling temperature, the only downside to my plan is all the time I have to think. What I'm about to do is as simple as can be, so there's no real point in visualizing it too many times. It's more a matter of having balls at the right time than working out the details. I watch the front door and drift into a state of thoughtful introspection.

Cordoba's dead. Ella wants to commit me. This is the last day of my life.

Lisa would have plenty to say about this.

—*You're obsessing. Walk away.*

—*No.*

—*You need help.*

—*Get a gun and help, then.*

—*You got your memories back. Wasn't that the point? You won.*

—*I won, but I'm not even.*

—*You'll go to jail.*

—*No, I won't.*

—*I'm not worth it.*

—*Who said anything about you?*
—*Christian. This won't change anything.*
—*This will change everything.*
—*It won't change us.*
—*We'll see about that.*

I go through an infinite number of variations of this conversation, all of which end up as the same unresolved agita burning up the center of my chest. Lisa's voice in my head has taken on a tone that's more sedate than argumentative. The simple unsolicited wisdom of someone who can see what's coming but can do nothing to change it.

It's got to be close to eleven forty-five by now. Just about time for the midnight shift change. I think I'm freezing. I rub my hands together for five minutes straight to limber them up in case I have to pull a trigger. I should spend a little time in a coffee shop to get this cold out of my bones, but that would mean I take my eye off the front door for more than ten seconds and I can't do that. Not now. Oh no, no, no.

Ah ha.

There he is, the fat fuck. Same mustache. Same self-important walk. Thirty years later, sixty pounds heavier, and gray. Looks like he made detective. I wonder which came first, the promotion or the belly. He stops on the sidewalk to finish up his conversation with the uniform he walked out with.

No point in waiting. I give my hands one last good rub, bend and stretch them a few times, and decide they're ready.

I cross the street as he wraps it up with the uniform. I slip behind him on the sidewalk as he heads down West Tenth Street. Whistling. Still with the whistling. Could I ever be so self-satisfied that I whistle to myself for the sheer joy of it?

Maybe someone is watching. Probably Goose is packing. Definitely there are cops around. I pull the Glock out and get a nice firm grip on it. It feels so solid in my hand. I should walk around with one of these all the time. The weight and the design are so reassuring. This is my new best friend.

—Hey.

Whistling.

—DeMare.

Now I know he knows two things. He's a seasoned cop so he heard me the first time and decided not to turn around. Figured I'm calling to someone else, which means it's not his problem. When I used his last name he knew I'm looking for him specifically and that my tone means this will not be a social conversation. He keeps walking but I know that's because he's waiting for me to do something stupid. My heart is racing because I know this is the right thing to do. I've never been more focused.

—I'm Tony's boy.

That must have been stupid enough because he stops and turns his mustache around to face me. He squints and thinks and finally nods. I looked a lot like my father before I ruined my body. Maybe there was some of that left.

That god damn smirk.

—Hey, look at the big shot.

I can't tell if he's noticed the gun I'm holding next to my leg or doesn't care. He must have seen it. No way a guy on the job this long misses it. He doesn't think I'll use it. His chubby arms hang by his side like they have nothing better to do. There is no flinch in him. It might not be the first time someone approached him holding a gun.

—What's up?

I finger the Glock and notice the handle is slick with sweat. When did this thing get so heavy?

—Whaddaya want, kid? Put the gun down and tell me.

—I know what you did.

I thought it would feel different to say it out loud.

His voice is calm, but he's calculating things like how dilated my pupils are, how fast he can draw his gun, and whether it's possible or even worth it to talk me out of what I'm about to do.

—Yeah, so? It was a long time ago. Besides, I didn't do nothing. Your dad did everything. Read the papers.

Five hours of rehearsal and I can't lift my arm. He's waiting for me to play my part in this scene. I can't.

No. Not can't. Don't. I don't lift my arm. I don't take aim. I don't do what Goose thinks I'm going to do. I don't.

I see you, Goose. Not the eyes on your face. Not the you that you think you are. I'm looking through you and you're long gone. You're gone like my mother and my father and my eight-year-old self. You're gone, Goose. Like everything else.

Tension streams from my pores, releasing itself on its own recognizance. I can't feel my hands. I'm sinking and soaring at the same time. I don't even know if my heart is beating anymore.

What I am not is afraid.

I watch old Goose with my aching eyes and Goose watches me, both of us so still. He, sizing me up. Me, transcending.

Goose, I had such high hopes for you. For us. The plan was to go out together. A blaze of glory. A yin and yang of cause and effect. Revenge and comeuppance. Absolution all around. But that's not going to happen now.

If my muscles relax anymore, I'll melt right out of these clothes. I am serenity. I think I might be floating. I may have dropped the gun.

I can see the glow behind your head, Goose. I know what's coming. It's the same light I would find if I opened my chest cavity and looked in. If you've ever seen a white star, you know exactly what I'm talking about. That's the one that burns the brightest. It's a chaste white light. Unsullied. Welcoming. It's the same light that grows behind me as I explain this to you. I know it's there. If you could see it, you'd be blinded by now. But you can't. That's my light, Goose. It's for me.

I don't know if he tackled me or watched me leave or called for backup or decided I was a harmless crackpot and walked away. By the time I turned around to see the new world behind me I had forgotten Goose and karma and living and breathing and hanging and punching and needles. I didn't need them anymore. When I turned around, what I found was The White.

And I walked right into it.

84

White.

The White.

I'm back. I've never felt better in my life.
Unsplintered.
Whole.
This is where I belong.
The Whoosh begins and I feel relaxed. My old friend. The memories wash over me and I fall in love with each and every one of them all over again. Only this time I go with them, swimming in and out, up and down, alongside them in perfect sync.

Look at me, Lisa. I did it. I'm whole again. Forever. I'm perfect.
We're perfect.
I know I'll never leave here and I know that's the way it should be.
This is me.
I am The White.

White.